"Sure," Kuming agreed, then suddenly thrust his arms forward and opened his fists. Two steel balls flew from his hands, and the metal spheres struck Manning in the chest. He stumbled backward, triggering the FAL in his fists.

Kuming lunged and seized the FAL. He pulled hard and turned sharply, tearing the rifle from Manning's hands. The momentum threw the Phoenix Force warrior off-balance, and he hurtled awkwardly into a leather armchair. Man and furniture toppled in a helpless heap. Gripping the rifle by its barrel and wielding it like a club, Kuming advanced on Manning.

Encizo whirled around to help, but the other yakuza thug, Tanaka, lashed out with the *manrikigusari*. The weapon's steel links spun around Encizo's ankles, and the weighted end locked around the length of the chain. Tanaka tugged swiftly on the chain, yanking the Cuban's feet from under him and sending him crashing to the floor with a violent thud.

"Eat this, spic," Tanaka snarled as he raised his foot to stomp his heel into Encizo's face.

Mack Bolan's
PHOENIX FORCE

PHOENIX FORCE

Ninja Blood

Gar Wilson

A GOLD EAGLE BOOK FROM

TORONTO • NEW YORK • LONDON • PARIS
AMSTERDAM • STOCKHOLM • HAMBURG
ATHENS • MILAN • TOKYO • SYDNEY

First edition January 1988

ISBN 0-373-61333-4

Special thanks and acknowledgment to
William Fieldhouse for his contribution to this work.

Printed in Canada

1

Nagano Jiro should have been a very happy man. He was the executive vice president of Kin-Rakooda, one of Japan's top ten automobile manufacturers, which was rapidly increasing its production and sales. Nagano earned a large salary, he lived with his beautiful wife in a big house at the outskirts of Kyoto, and he could afford champagne for breakfast or to fly to Paris for lunch. He should have felt as though he had the world by the tail.

But Nagano Jiro had a problem, a problem that could cost him his life. Since he had the means, he took precautions to protect himself. His limousine was constructed of reinforced steel and bulletproof glass. He traveled with three armed bodyguards and carried a Nambu 9 mm autoloading pistol.

Nagano was speeding away from Kyoto in his limousine. One of the bodyguards drove, while he sat with his other protectors in the back. The vice president of Kin-Rakooda nervously took a pack of cigarettes from his jacket. He had become a chronic chain-smoker and put away three packs a day. He suspected he might be getting an ulcer, but consider-

ing the other threats to his health, that hardly seemed
to matter.

"Dozo, Nagano-san," one of the bodyguards said
gently. "Please, Mr. Nagano. Try to relax. Nothing
will happen to you. We are here to see to that."

Nagano nodded, but he didn't share the man's con-
fidence. Former soldiers, the bodyguards were trained
to fight other soldiers in open combat. They were
skilled in jujitsu, karate and had learned combat-
shooting, escape and evasion techniques and security
procedures. But Nagano was familiar with the methods of his enemies, and he couldn't relax. The bodyguards followed rules and laws, but the enemy believed
in accomplishing their goals by any means possible,
and they weren't accustomed to failure.

The chauffeur steered the limo onto a side road,
avoiding the main traffic to and from Kyoto. The
headlights cut through the gloom as twilight gave way
to night. Peering through the rear window, Nagano
noticed a pair of headlights that seemed to be tailing
the limo.

"We're being followed!" Nagano exclaimed,
reaching for the Nambu pistol inside his jacket.

"Leave the gun in its holster, Nagano-*san*," one of
the bodyguards urged, figuring that a nervous ama-
teur with a gun was more of a liability than an asset in
an emergency. "Maybe it's just a car going the same
way we are."

The driver pushed the gas pedal, and the car behind them also accelerated to keep up with the big
black automobile. Nagano tensed, gripping the lapel

of his jacket so he could feel the reassuring bulge of the pistol. The fact that he was armed comforted him although he knew little more about guns than which end to hold.

The limousine moved faster, and the second car gained speed accordingly. The bodyguards prepared for trouble. One was poised to throw himself at Nagano to shield him, while the second one unbuttoned his jacket for easy access to his American-made .357 Magnum revolver. The chauffeur opened a compartment next to his seat. It contained a compact .380 caliber Ingram M-11 machine pistol.

The cars sped along the road. Traffic was very light, especially for early evening in Japan. A few cars and an occasional truck or bus headed in the opposite direction, toward Kyoto. The area was dotted with houses, split-level structures surrounded by bamboo fences. The families who lived there were middle class, near the upper crust. They could afford homes that offered some privacy, a cherished commodity in Japan. The sort of people who minded their own business and kept to themselves, they weren't given to gazing out windows at the road to watch the traffic passing by. If the pursuing car decided to ambush Nagano's vehicle, witnesses would probably notice few details.

"What are you doing?" Nagano demanded with alarm as the driver slowed the limo.

"I am trying to find out if the car behind us is really a threat," the chauffeur replied. "Please try to remain calm, sir."

"Hai," Nagano assured him, but he hadn't felt calm for nearly a week.

The chauffeur steered the limo toward the guard-rail along the side of the road. The other vehicle's driver honked his horn in protest and swerved, narrowly missing the limousine's left taillight, then continued down the road. The limo driver allowed another automobile to pass by before he accelerated to travel the road at a greater speed.

"You see, Nagano-*san*?" the chauffeur said cheerfully. "We were never in any danger, after all."

"I feel a bit foolish now," Nagano admitted, mopping his forehead with a silk handkerchief.

"The threats against your life may be hollow," one of the bodyguards remarked. "But it is best to consider any possible hazard as a genuine risk. Do not worry, Nagano-*san*. We will take care of you."

"Arigato," Nagano replied with a nod. He hadn't told them why he really felt he was in danger. The security agency had been informed that he had received several anonymous threats over the phone, but Nagano hadn't given any details about his plight.

The limo journeyed on without further incident. At last it approached the long paved driveway to Nagano's home. The house was surrounded by an iron fence three meters high, and a uniformed guard was stationed at the gate. The guard shack was equipped with a telephone with a direct line into the main house to screen visitors, an emergency alarm switch under the desk to contact the police and the controls to the electrically operated front gate.

As the limo approached, the gate slid open. Nagano noticed that the light in the guard shack was off, but he saw the outline of the sentry's flying saucer cap, perched on the man's head. The limousine rolled across the threshold and came to a halt by the shack so the guard could report what had occurred during his duty shift.

The chauffeur pressed a button to lower the bulletproof window at the passenger's side, and the guard stepped from his shack. In a split-second realization, the limo driver saw that the sentry wasn't in uniform but was clad in a black outfit with a scarf mask across his nose and mouth. The man's gloved fist held a pistol with a nine-inch sound suppressor attached to the barrel.

"Ninja!" the chauffeur gasped with alarm just before the phony guard squeezed the trigger. A .380-caliber bullet hissed from the silenced pistol and smashed into the driver's forehead.

One bodyguard immediately threw himself over Nagano to shield him with his own body. The other protector drew his Magnum revolver and opened the door at the driver's side of the car. Crouching, he shuffled from the limo, his gun held in a firm two-hand grip.

He barely heard the whine of the projectile that hurtled from the shadows surrounding the main house. The arrow struck him in the chest, the sharp tip sinking deep to puncture a lung. The wounded man cried out and slumped against the frame of the limo as blood oozed across his white shirt and narrow striped necktie.

The masked gunman had pumped two more bullets into the motionless chauffeur, who was almost certainly dead, but the assassin's training called for more bullets to make sure the victim wouldn't survive. Suddenly another black-clad shape appeared next to the gunman. The second assassin yanked the pin from a hand grenade and tossed it through the open window of the car, then the two figures in black ducked behind the guard shack.

The bodyguard inside the limo saw the grenade fly into the front seat, which was separated by a thick shatterproof sheet of glass from the rear compartment. He realized he couldn't lower the glass and reach the grenade in time to toss it from the vehicle before it exploded.

Scooping Nagano Jiro in his arms, he dove from the car, tumbling out the door his partner had used and dragging Nagano with him. Holding on to his employer, he was rolling away from the limo when the grenade exploded.

The armor-plated car contained the blast to a limited degree as the explosion smashed the vehicle from within. The glass burst apart, and the thick reinforced steel doors popped off their hinges. The blast punched through the dashboard to the engine block, severing the fuel line, and sparks ignited the gasoline. Flames danced along the undercarriage.

Shielding Nagano, the bodyguard groaned with pain as shards of metal shrapnel pierced his back. He started to rise, still hunched over to protect the executive.

An arrow streaked out from the shadows to hit the bodyguard's right side. The arrowhead pierced the flesh between his ribs and slid into the chest cavity. His howl of agony created an ugly gurgle as blood rose into his throat.

Nagano Jiro shoved his wounded protector aside and bolted in panic toward the house. The fire within the limo had spread rapidly through the fuel line to detonate the gas tank. The fuel exploded in the confined container, and the second blast hurled the limo into an awkward headstand. The big black car heaved up on its nose and crashed down on its tires as the flames crackled across mutilated steel and torn upholstery.

The second explosion caught Nagano off guard. He lost his footing and fell face first on the manicured lawn. Two feet, shod in black split-toe *tabi* slippers, appeared near Nagano's head. He trembled violently as he slowly raised his head to stare up at the sinister black shape that stood over his prone body.

"Ee-ya!" Nagano cried out when he saw the long curved steel blade in the assassin's fists.

The emotionless dark eyes above the black mask revealed that the ninja didn't intend to show any mercy. The sword swooped downward like a stroke of lightning. Sharp steel sliced through Nagano's neck as if it was made of soft clay. His body jerked and twitched in a wild muscular spasm, then rolled over, blood spitting from the stump of the neck. Nagano's head remained facedown in the grass.

The bodyguard with the arrow sticking from his chest dragged himself toward the swordsman. He wrenched the arrow from his chest, but the shaft snapped off against bone. Shrieking in agony, he managed to hold on to the .357 Magnum in his fist. His vision blurred as he raised the weapon.

His target suddenly vanished, bolting behind the cover of a large marble sundial. The bodyguard pulled the trigger. His revolver roared, streaking an orange flame into the night. The recoil shoved his arm toward the sky, and the Magnum nearly jumped out of his grasp. He cursed under his breath, aware that he had missed the sword-wielding killer by more than two yards.

Unexpectedly, another black-suited assassin jumped him from behind. Strong fingers seized his wrist and twisted hard to force the revolver from his grasp. He turned to face his opponent. Dark almond-shaped eyes glared above the black-mask. He raised his left hand to deliver a karate chop at the killer's face.

A terrible pain raked through his nervous system as sharp steel plunged into his solar plexus. Piercing deep into his chest, the blade sliced tissue and carved upward into the xiphoid process at the bottom of the sternum, then the tip stabbed his heart. He struck out desperately with his hand, hoping to kill his tormentor with a blow to the neck.

The side of his hand chopped the assassin across the face. The ninja groaned and retreated from his victim, both hands reaching for the broken cartilage at the bridge of his nose.

"Son of a bitch," the killer rasped in English as blood began to soak into his mask. He swung a vicious kick between the splayed legs of the bodyguard, hoping that the man lived long enough to feel his testicles smash into a pulp. He was distracted by the wail of sirens announcing that the police had been alerted and at least one squad car was headed toward the site.

The black-suited killers didn't want to confront the police. They had accomplished their mission for the night, and it was time to leave.

Four shadowy figures dashed through the open gate and piled into the back of the Toyota pickup truck that had rolled up to the driveway. The truck raced from the scene, heading north as the police approached from the south. Their escape had been planned in advance. Stolen earlier that night, the Toyota would be abandoned after they were clear of the scene. After a change of clothes, they would disperse in other vehicles.

"Do shi-mashita?" one of the assassins asked when he noticed his comrade's mask was stained with crimson.

"Bastard broke my fuckin' nose, that's what's wrong," the other ninja replied with a dull groan.

The questioner didn't understand English, so he simply nodded.

2

"Well, judging by that mission in Spain, you've certainly fully recovered, Yakov," Hal Brognola, the head Fed, announced as he watched the five men of Phoenix Force file into the War Room.

"And it had been none too soon," Yakov Katzenelenbogen replied with a smile. "I was ready to go back to work."

The unit commander of Phoenix Force had spent time recuperating in a hospital from an injury caused by an explosion. He had been temporarily blinded, and there had been concern about his eyesight. The Force, in the meantime, had plunged leaderless into an assignment in Kenya. But by the time of the Spanish mission, Katz had been raring to go.

"I've seen your score at the firing range this morning," Brognola remarked, glancing down at a report form on the table next to a stack of file folders. "Pretty impressive shooting, Yakov. Nothing wrong with your eyes now?"

"Not a thing, Hal," Katz assured him. "And I can see you've had some work piling up on your desk lately."

He gestured at the file folders, pointing with the trident hook device at the end of his right arm. Katz's arm had been amputated at the elbow following a near-fatal explosion that had mangled the limb beyond repair and killed Katz's personal aide—who also happened to be his only son.

The tragedy had occurred while Katz fought with the Israeli forces during the Six Day War. It had been one of many battlefields he had survived since he joined the French Resistance when still a teenager. That was the start of a career in espionage, intelligence operations and every conceivable form of combat that would continue for more than four decades.

The American OSS soon took an interest in Katz, and they enlisted him for new assignments behind enemy lines. By the end of World War II, Yakov Katzenelenbogen was a seasoned veteran, highly respected for his intelligence and skills.

Katz moved to Palestine after the war and became involved in Israel's struggle for independence. He became the most valuable intelligence officer in Mossad, Israel's efficient, and frequently quite ruthless, spy network.

Katz was something of a legend in the shadowy world of espionage, although only a handful of people knew his true name. Due to his unique background and language skills—which came to include Hebrew and Arabic—he was in great demand. He served with the American CIA, the West German BND, the French Sûreté and the British SIS.

But Katz's incredible career reached a new high point when he was selected as the team leader for Phoenix Force. The five-man unit was comprised of the best antiterrorist commandos and most highly skilled combat specialists in the free world.

Katz didn't look much like a veteran soldier. Slightly overweight and middle-aged, he seemed to be a scholarly gray-haired gentleman with a gentle smile and expressive blue eyes. Yet the one-armed former Mossad colonel was one of the best-trained and most experienced experts in his field.

"We've got a job for you guys, but you might not want to take this mission," Brognola began, taking a cigar from his shirt pocket. "Did you happen to hear a news item about the murder of a Japanese auto executive?"

"I heard something about it on the car radio this morning," Gary Manning remarked as he slid into a chair at the table. "Pretty brief commentary, and I didn't really listen that close. News report said the guy was the vice president of an auto corporation I'd never heard of before. They said the murder appeared to be a mob hit by Japanese gangsters."

Manning was a big guy, less than six feet tall, but built like a lumberjack from his native Canada. A long-distance runner, weight-lifter and superb rifle marksman, Manning was a patient man and possessed uncanny endurance, both physical and mental.

He was also one of the best explosives experts in the world. Such work requires nerves of steel, hands as steady as a brain surgeon's and the ability to remain calm even if the sky threatens to burst into flames and fall. Manning possessed all the qualifications, and a lot more.

He had been a lieutenant when the Canadian armed forces offered him a chance to go to Vietnam as a "special observer" attached to the Fifth Special Forces. He accepted the challenge and learned a lot during his tour in Vietnam. Although intelligent and realistic, the young Canadian had been naive about the reality of actual combat, but the grim facts of jungle warfare soon dispelled any dreams of glory. He learned to use his demolition skills with deadly efficiency and became a first-class sniper. Most important, Manning learned how to survive.

He was awarded the Silver Star, one of the few Canadian citizens to receive that honor during the Vietnam conflict. After he returned to Canada, the intelligence section of the Royal Canadian Mounted Police enlisted Manning. Part of Manning's training included an assignment to West Germany, where he was attached to the newly formed GSG-9, an elite antiterrorist squad.

After his time in Germany, Manning returned to Canada to discover that the RCMP had been put out of the intelligence business. The newly formed Canadian Security Intelligence Service offered Manning a desk job, but he decided to go into the business world instead. He became an executive with North American International and was on his way to becoming president of the firm, but the invitation to become part of Phoenix Force was too strong a lure for the rugged Canadian to refuse.

"Japanese gangsters?" Rafael Encizo raised his black eyebrows. "So the guy was killed by yakuza, the Japanese Mafia outfits. Probably means he was yakuza himself. Pretty rare for them to kill civilians...unless this auto executive was causing some sort of problems."

"The bio on—" Hal Brognola checked his files to read the dead man's name "—Nagano Jiro, I think that's how it's pronounced. Anyway, there isn't much about the guy in the bio we got from Kompei intelligence in Japan. What we have suggests Nagano probably was connected with some yakuza clan. A lot of high-level businessmen and government officials in Japan are connected with the yakuza, you know."

"So a hood got killed by some other hoods," Encizo said with a shrug. "Sorry if I can't get too excited about that, Hal. Innocent people are victims all the time. I feel a lot worse about them."

The muscular, good-looking Cuban warrior had seen a lot of suffering. Most of his family, though not politically involved, had been killed during the Communist takeover in his homeland.

The courageous teenager then joined a band of resistance fighters to combat the Communists with guerrilla warfare. But the young freedom fighters were inexperienced, and soon most of Encizo's friends were dead. Young Rafael and a few other survivors managed to flee to the United States.

On April 17, 1961, Encizo returned to Cuba as part of the abortive Bay of Pigs invasion. Many of the would-be liberators were killed, and Encizo was taken prisoner. He was sent to El Principe, Castro's notorious political prison. Encizo was starved, beaten and tortured, yet he didn't break.

He gradually pretended to endorse the dogma of his captors. They ceased the physical mistreatment, and Encizo was treated better as a reward for being cooperative. The rest and decent food allowed him to regain enough strength to break the neck of a careless guard and escape from prison.

Returning to the United States, he became a naturalized citizen and worked in numerous professions, including scuba diving, and as a professional bodyguard and an insurance investigator. Encizo had dived for sunken treasure, and assisted the FBI and DEA in combating drug smugglers and organized crime.

But Encizo seldom worked at any job for more than a year. No matter how unusual or challenging the task seemed in the beginning, he always tired of the monotony that eventually accompanies any duty. When the Cuban was offered the opportunity to join Phoenix Force, he accepted the new challenge and found that the missions assigned to the unit were anything but dull.

"Rafael's got a point," David McCarter commented as he fired up a Player's cigarette. "Yakuza killing yakuza isn't exactly unique news. A couple years ago the Japanese gangsters were killing each other in the streets of Tokyo in broad daylight. They had a little war going. Sort of an Asian version of *The Godfather*. I don't recall anybody getting too excited about that being a threat to national security. I don't see what a yakuza assassination has to do with Phoenix Force.''

''It's not just the yakuza we're worried about,'' Brognola replied grimly.

''So it's those crazy buggers from TRIO again,'' McCarter snorted. ''When the hell is Interpol going to start paying attention to those bastards and do some bleeding work for a change?''

Patience had never been one of David McCarter's virtues. Neither was keeping his mouth shut and listening before making remarks about something without hearing all the facts. The tall fox-faced Briton tended to get a bit surly just before a mission. He was eager to get into the field.

McCarter was a product of the rough-and-tumble streets of East London. He had thrived in a tough environment and never seemed interested in making things much easier for himself.

David McCarter's personal goals were quite simple. He wanted to experience excitement and adventure, and to satisfy his appetite, he joined the British army and became a member of the elite Special Air Service.

McCarter's duties with SAS had ranged from being a ''special observer'' in Vietnam to stalking IRA terrorists in Northern Ireland. He had been assigned to Oman during the conflicts with the Marxist guerrillas in the Dhofar region in the 1970s. McCarter even participated in a covert SAS "police action" in Hong Kong, and he was among the SAS commandos to successfully storm the Iranian Embassy in London during the spectacular 1980 Operation Nimrod raid.

The gutsy Briton was an ideal choice for Phoenix Force, and since the Force received only the most difficult and dangerous assignments, McCarter had been eager to join.

"Actually," Brognola commented, leafing through the file folders on the table, "we don't know if TRIO is involved or not. Even if TRIO is responsible, the crime was committed in Japan against Japanese citizens—three of Nagano's bodyguards were also killed. Anyway, jurisdiction is definitely in the court of the Japanese authorities. We wouldn't take any interest in this case if it wasn't for two bits of information."

Brognola chewed his unlit cigar as he passed some report forms to Katz. These included grisly photographs of the decapitated body of Nagano Jiro and his slain bodyguards, as well as eyewitness reports by Nagano's wife and servants, who had seen the murders from the windows of their home.

"You'll notice that the witnesses described the assassins as dressed in black clothing with scarf masks covering their lower faces. I don't have to tell you guys that sounds like the traditional costume of a ninja. You've come up against ninja before. You know they still use traditional weapons as well as modern firearms and explosives. Nagano was decapitated by a sword. Two of his bodyguards were shot by a bow and arrow. One of them was finished off with a knife, and the blade was still sticking in the guy's chest when the cops arrived. It was a Cold Steel Tanto, a knife combining the old Japanese samurai knife with modern steel alloys and rubberized nonslip grips on the handle. You're familiar with this knife, Rafael.''

"Sure," Encizo confirmed with a nod. "I've carried a Cold Steel Tanto into combat lots of times. It's an excellent weapon, and I've used it in enough knife fights to know. I also think I'm beginning to understand why we're getting involved in this multiple-murder case in Japan. The Cold Steel Tanto is made here in the United States.''

"Right," Brognola said. "And that suggests that at least one of the ninja assassins was from America. Now, before you guys left for Kenya on your last mission, you might recall we had a brief conversation about John Trent.''

"Yeah," Calvin James replied, giving Brognola a hard look. "You said we couldn't enlist Trent for the Kenya mission because he was in Japan and nobody was sure where he was staying or what he was doing there. You also hinted that all of a sudden Stony Man doesn't trust the guy anymore.''

"Trent is an American, trained as a ninja," the Fed stated. "There aren't very many of those around. Now, we've got evidence that an American ninja participated in the murder of a noted Japanese industrialist. It's an interesting coincidence that Trent just happens to be in Japan at the time.''

"Wait a minute, Hal," James began. "I've known John longer than anybody in this room. I don't believe he'd work as a hired killer for the yakuza."

A tall athletic black man, Calvin James was the most recent recruit of Phoenix Force, although he was hardly a newcomer and had participated in two-thirds of their missions. James had replaced Keio Ohara, the original fifth member of Phoenix Force who had been killed in action.

James was the only native-born American of the team, and it's youngest member. He had been born and raised in the South side of Chicago. It wasn't an easy place to grow up.

There are only a few ways of getting out of the ghetto, unless one is gifted as an entertainer, athlete or with a near-genuis IQ. James was a good athlete, but not quite good enough for pro ball, and he had seen too many pro-boxer hopefuls on skid row with their brains scrambled. James was good with his fists, but he wasn't going to try to punch his way to fortune.

He was smart and his grades in school had been better than average, but not high enough to have any college beg him to enroll and offer a discount scholarship. A lot of kids in Calvin's position turned to crime, but he wanted no part of that corruption.

Enlisting into the Navy at the age of seventeen, he became a hospital corpsman. His physical abilities, intelligence and prowess with weapons led to his recruitment with SEALs—Sea, Air and Land teams. He served in Vietnam where he was decorated for courage and dedication beyond the call of duty.

After Nam, James returned to the States and pursued a career in medicine and chemistry by enrolling at UCLA on the GI bill. His goals changed after his mother was murdered by muggers and his kid sister died from an overdose of heroin.

James joined the San Francisco Police Department because he wanted to combat crime, and the Chicago PD would never have accepted him on the force when they learned what happened to his family.

However, James's personality wasn't suitable for standard police work, and the SFPD soon realized that a man with James's skills didn't belong in a squad car patrolling the neighborhood. So James was invited to join the Special Weapons and Tactics squad. He was still a SWAT team member when Phoenix Force drafted him into his first mission with the elite commando unit. He had remained with them ever since.

Phoenix Force was the ultimate special-operations outfit. Its members were the very best experts in their field. Originally assembled by Stony Man, the Force's first five members had been personally selected by Mack Bolan himself. Phoenix Force had been created to combat international terrorism, but over the years targets had expanded to include organized crime, enemy espionage and various types of conspiracies that threatened the welfare of the United States. Hal Brognola, head of the Sensitive Operations Group, and Stony Man, liaison with the Oval Office, gave them their assignments. The only other boss they had was the President of the United States, and even he didn't know any details about Phoenix Force except those that Brognola saw fit to give him.

"Look, Cal," Brognola said with a sigh. "None of us *want* to believe Trent is working for the yakuza syndicate, but we can't ignore the evidence that suggests Trent has become a hit man for the Japanese mob."

"There's no solid evidence John is a blasted hired killer," James insisted. "For pity's sake, Hal. You're talking about a guy who joined Phoenix Force on three missions. Trent put his ass on the line for us. He risked his life on more than one occasion for the success of each mission."

"I agree with Cal," McCarter stated as he rose from his chair and started to pace. The Briton could never stay seated for long. "Trent fought side by side with us. On two missions we were up against TRIO, and that included yakuza that are part of that outfit. The bloke isn't a bloody hoodlum."

"Unfortunately," Brognola stated, "we don't know that."

"Hal," James said in a frustrated tone, "I knew John Trent when I was still a cop back in Frisco. I can vouch for his loyalty."

"Did Trent ever tell you about his uncle?" the Fed asked, scanning the contents of another file folder. "A guy named Inoshiro Nakezuri? His sister was married to Victor Trent, John's father. Pretty good chance Inoshiro introduced his nephew to *ninjutsu*. We figure Inoshiro was a ninja himself."

"Yeah," James said, rolling his eyes toward the ceiling. "John told me about his uncle. I even met Inoshiro once. The old guy runs a television repair shop in San Francisco."

"That's a front," Brognola declared, sliding the report across the table to James. "Inoshiro is a member of the yakuza. In fact, he's a subchief of the Kaiju Clan that has been active in the United States for more than ten years."

"I thought the Kaiju Clan was the ninja clan Trent belonged to," Gary Manning remarked.

"Maybe they were ninja once, but they're yakuza now," the Fed explained. "I was shocked when this information reached my desk last week. It made Trent's reliability questionable, to say the least."

"Hell," James groaned after glancing at the report on Inoshiro. "It says here that John's uncle has been involved in bootleg videotapes, phony Rolex watches, a little black market in TV sets and cameras, that kind of chicken shit stuff. You make it sound as if he's a Japanese Al Capone."

Brognola gave them a rueful look. "That's all the feds have found out so far about Inoshiro. Under the circumstances, we have to assume the worst and figure Trent may very well be working for the yakuza—as a professional assassin."

"I hate to say this," Katz told the others, "but Hal is right. We can't assume Trent is innocent simply because we like him and he's worked with us on previous missions."

"Yeah," Encizo agreed reluctantly. "Trent's loyalty to his uncle and the Kaiju could be greater than any sense of patriotism. Besides, killing a Japanese businessman isn't a threat to American national security. Maybe he could justify it that way."

"But Trent could be a threat to national security," Brognola said as he shoved the cigar into the corner of his mouth. "He knows about Phoenix Force—maybe not by name—and he has no details about Stony Man, but Trent is one of the few people who knows all five of you by your real names. He is also acquainted with details of the three missions he participated in."

"If he's working for a yakuza clan, the leaders might realize information about us could be sold or traded to TRIO," Katz remarked. "I'm sure we're already on TRIO's death list, and knowing our real names would make it easier for TRIO to hunt us down."

"The situation won't be much better if the police or Kompei Special Internal Affairs nail Trent," Brognola added. "The press will talk to him if the cops get him. Trent could tell them all about Phoenix Force being involved in operations in San Francisco and Hong Kong, not to mention that business at the Vatican about a year and a half ago. That incident was world news, and investigative journalists are still trying to find out what really happened at the Vatican. The publicity would cripple us, and the President would probably order us to disband at least temporarily."

"And if Kompei gets Trent that means he could give all the information about us to the Japanese secret service," Encizo commented. "Japan and the United States are still on friendly terms, and we're pretty strong allies, so that would probably be a better situation than any other alternative we've discussed so far. It would still be a big problem for Uncle Sam because Kompei would probably figure that Trent was some sort of government assassin that the U.S. had lost control of. Definitely wouldn't improve foreign relations, and it would put us in hot water for sure."

"That's right," Brognola confirmed. "That's why you guys are going to Japan as soon as possible. You remember Ken Ikeda, chief of Kompei Special Internal Affairs?"

"Who?" Calvin James asked, totally confused.

"We worked with Ikeda on a mission before you were part of the team," Gary Manning explained. "That was the Japanese Red Cell terrorist mess back...oh, must have been about four years ago."

Brognola nodded. "Right. You'll be working with him again. Of course, that means Kompei will know why you're looking for Trent, but that will also cancel out the possibility of Kompei accusing the U.S. of letting an American ninja assassin run around Japan killing people. I'd rather not bring Kompei into this, but you'd never have a chance of finding Trent in a densely populated country like Japan without professional help."

"He might not be so easy to find, anyway," Manning commented. "Trent is a ninja. The art of *ninjutsu* is one of stealth and invisibility."

"I don't have to remind any of you guys that Trent is potentially as dangerous as any opponent you've come up against in the past," the Fed stated. "You've seen him in action before."

"Ninja are always dangerous," McCarter remarked. "And Trent is the best-trained ninja we've ever encountered."

"Wait a minute," James insisted. "I still think John's innocent of these charges that he's a yakuza killer."

"That'll be fine with me," Brognola assured him. "But you'd better find proof that he isn't, because things don't look so good for him now. If it turns out that Trent is working for the yakuza we can't afford to let him talk."

"You want us to kill him?" Katz asked directly.

"We can't afford to let him talk," Brognola repeated. "Draw your own conclusions."

3

The two yakuza thugs were big men by Japanese standards. Trent was slightly taller than either man, but both thugs were dedicated weight lifters, and their muscle bulk was much greater than that of the slender American. Trent thought that the yakuza looked uncomfortable in their expensive business suits and neckties. Their preferred clothing probably would be casual or loin cloths made from the hides of wild animals.

The two had met Trent in the lobby of the Yoee-Uma Import-Export Company's office building, one of hundreds on Exchange Avenue in downtown Tokyo. The muscle boys had escorted Trent from the spacious lobby to the elevators. They frisked him during the trip up to the tenth floor. The only weapon he carried was a *metsubushi*, a hollowed-out eggshell filled with black pepper. Trent hadn't even added any flash powder to the *metsubushi* because he hadn't been able to purchase any while in Japan. He had handed over the egg without argument. The two gorillas were amused by the *metsubushi* and joked about it as they traveled up the elevator shaft. One of them opened his jacket to show Trent a 9 mm Walther P-38 in shoulder leather.

"This shoots little eggs called bullets," the thug snickered. "They are better than your egg."

"Hai," Trent agreed. "Those little eggs are much better."

"Why did you bring this thing if you wish to speak peacefully with Kaiju-*san*?" the other gorilla demanded.

"The streets of Tokyo are like those of any other major city," Trent answered. "Potentially dangerous."

"Every place is dangerous these days," the thug replied.

Trent's belt was made of thick leather with a large oval buckle of stainless steel covered by black enamel. It could be used as a weapon in an emergency, but Trent realized it was no match for a gun. He hadn't come to Japan to harm Kaiju Hideo. Trent hoped he could indeed resolve his problem peacefully.

The elevator opened, and the thugs led Trent through the immaculate corridor to the office of Kaiju Hideo, the president of Yoee-Uma. Two young secretaries, pretty enough to be professional models, nodded as the three men entered the front office. The women rose and left their desks, heading for the hallway. Apparently, Kaiju had already informed them that he wanted the meeting to be private.

One of the thugs opened the thick walnut door to the main office. The room was almost thirty feet across, with a wet bar, a stereo system and a large color television set. Kaiju Hideo sat behind a wide Plexiglas desk with a black and white phone next to a slotted tray for mail. The desk was bare except for a gooseneck lamp and a set of gold-plated pens jutting from a black onyx base.

Kaiju was a short, thickly built man with hard black eyes and a frown engraved on his wide face. His hair was gray at the temples, and a fold of loose skin hung over the collar of his pale blue shirt, nearly concealing the knot of his houndstooth necktie.

Trent noticed the bookshelves behind Kaiju's desk. *The Temple of the Golden Pavilion* and several other works by the late Yukio Mishima were among Kaiju's collection. There were also several books in English and a few in French. Next to the bookshelves stood a *katana* samurai sword in a vertical stand. Kaiju claimed he was descended from a noble samurai family. That was a lie, one of many that Kaiju endorsed.

The two muscle men bowed deeply to their employer, an expression of respect. Trent placed a hand on his knee and bent deeply from the waist, his right arm extended with the palm held up. It was the ceremonial salutation of the yakuza.

His head bowed, Trent intoned a formal Japanese greeting.

"Your manners at least are acceptable," Kaiju stated with a curt nod. "So you're Trent, the halfbreed son of Nakezuri Reko, Inoshiro's sister. Your father was an American soldier of the occupying troops in Tokyo after the war, correct?"

"Hai, Kaiju-san," Trent confirmed.

Let's get straight to business. I assume you represent your uncle Inoshiro.''

"That is correct,'' Trent answered.

"But you are not yakuza,'' Kaiju remarked. "Or have you finally decided to join us, after all?''

"No,'' Trent replied. "I am a *sensei*, an instructor in martial arts at a dojo in San Francisco. The work is rewarding, and I have no desire to branch off into forms of business that may lead to complications with the law. Not that I mean any disrespect toward you or the Kaiju Clan.''

"I'm so glad,'' Kaiju said with contempt. "Does your uncle fail to clearly understand the demands we have concerning the future of the Kaiju Clan? I want him to begin dealing in the sale of cocaine, marijuana and other drugs as soon as possible. The profit from minor-league black market is not great enough to merit continuing Inoshiro's branch of the clan. He must move on to dealing in products that offer more generous profits for the clan.''

"My uncle cannot oblige this request, Kaiju-*san*,'' Trent explained. "He has no wish to cause harm to others....''

"Your uncle does not understand,'' Kaiju said sharply. "I am not making a 'request,' Trent. I am giving Inoshiro an order. I expect that command to be obeyed.''

"You ask my uncle to dishonor himself,'' Trent declared. "His dealing in black market is illegal, but harms no one...at least not physically. Narcotics are a different matter.''

"I don't like Americans very much," Kaij[?] marked with a bored sigh. "I like their money. T[?] good, at least."

He examined Trent with a cold, critical eye. T[?] American was roughly six feet tall, with a lean build The almond shape of his brown eyes revealed his Japanese blood tie to the Nakezuri family. Kaiju's gaze lingered on Trent's hands. Calluses on the knuckles revealed training with a *makiwara*, a device used to temper hands for karate. Trent wore loose-fitting trousers and a cheap sports coat with a white shirt and a clip-on maroon tie. He was dressed in a manner that allowed ease of movement for swift action, if necessary. Trent had obviously thought he might have to fight. The tie was a precaution. If a man grabs a clip-on tie, he can't use it to pull an opponent off balance or choke him by yanking it over a shoulder. Kaiju wasn't impressed. If Trent thought he could survive a fight with Kaiju in his own office building, the American was either an egotistic moron or insane.

"You speak Japanese well for an American," Kaiju remarked.

"Domoarigato," Trent replied, expressing the most polite form of thanks. "I was raised in Japan until I was eighteen. I learned English and Japanese simultaneously."

"I see," Kaiju said with a yawn. That was very impolite and was meant to show that he was bored with the American. "I'm really a busy man, Trent-*san*.

"I don't intend to listen to you whine even if you are repeating the weak-stomached complaints of your uncle," the yakuza boss told him. "Inoshiro will lose his honor only if he refuses to obey me."

"Your demand is without honor," Trent told him. "And only a man without honor would make such a demand of my uncle. In America we would call you 'a real piece of shit,' Kaiju-*san*. I hope your English is good enough to understand the expression."

"You half-caste bastard!" Kaiju snarled, jumping from his seat. "How dare you come into my office and...behave so rudely!"

"Good manners are a waste of time with a piece of shit," Trent replied. "I think I ought to flush you instead."

One of the thugs reached inside his jacket for his gun, and the other stepped forward, apparently confident he could handle a mere American without a weapon. Trent caught their motion via the corner of an eye. He rapidly shuffled toward the man who presented the greatest threat—the one who was about to draw his gun.

Trent closed in quickly, startling the yakuza who was trying to clear his pistol from the jacket. The American whipped a back fist to the thug's face. The hood's head snapped back from the blow as he yanked the gun free. Trent chopped a hammer-fist stroke to the ulnar nerve in the guy's forearm. The pistol dropped from quivering, numb fingers.

The second thug launched a karate chop at Trent's neck, but the American blocked the attack with a rising forearm stroke and thrust the stiffened fingers of his other hand under the goon's rib cage. The man groaned as the stabbing fingers seemed to penetrate his lungs, driving the breath from his body. Trent hooked the heel of his left hand into the side of his opponent's jaw and followed with another right-hand palm stroke to the solar plexus.

The goon doubled up with a ragged gasp. Trent glanced at Kaiju and noticed that the yakuza leader was reaching for something concealed behind some phony books on the bookshelves. Probably a gun, Trent thought. He quickly grabbed the dazed hoodlum by an arm, locking it at the wrist and elbow. He ran toward the desk, pulling the thug forward. The flunky had no choice but to move with Trent unless he wanted his arm broken.

Trent stopped suddenly, turned slightly and shoved with both hands. He released the hood's arm and sent the thug hurtling into Kaiju's desk. The guy slid across the desk top and crashed into Kaiju. Both men fell to the floor.

The other goon had recovered from the back fist stroke and reached down to retrieve his pistol. Trent hadn't forgotten about him. The American dashed forward and lashed a kick to the man's face. The yakuza muscle man fell on his back with a groan, and Trent swept his other foot into the gun to kick it across the floor, toward the desk.

Trent dove after the gun, scooping up the Walther P-38 as he executed a fast shoulder roll. He landed in a kneeling position, with the pistol pointed at the two men behind the desk. Kaiju raised his empty hands in surrender, but his flunky swung a Nambu pistol toward Trent. The American snapped the Walther's safety catch, aimed and fired. A 9 mm parabellum tore into the chest of the yakuza goon. The man grunted and pulled the trigger of his Nambu. Trent stiffened with fear, expecting a bullet to smash into his flesh. The enemy's weapon didn't fire.

"Forgot to take the safety off, huh?" Trent muttered as he shot the thug again, pumping a bullet through his heart.

Trent turned the Walther toward Kaiju, but the yakuza boss had grabbed the swivel chair behind his desk and hurled it at Trent. The American ducked to avoid the flying piece of furniture, but a metal leg struck his shoulder and knocked him on his back. Kaiju rushed forward and kicked the gun from Trent's hand.

The American lashed out with a foot that connected with Kaiju's ribs. The yakuza chief staggered away from Trent, and the ninja sprang to his feet. The surviving henchman charged toward Trent and launched a *seiken* karate punch to Trent's jaw. The blow sent Trent stumbling backward into Kaiju.

The yakuza boss chopped the side of his hand between Trent's shoulder blades. Fortunately for the American, Kaiju wasn't skilled in karate and simply executed a technique he had seen in films. The blow was still hard enough to knock Trent toward the angry thug who was ready to deal another blow.

Trent suddenly dropped to one knee as the gorilla threw another punch. The fist shot above Trent's head, and the American quickly rammed an uppercut between his opponent's legs. The hood wheezed in agony as his testicles were mashed in by the *seiken* punch. Trent bolted upright, lashed a back kick into Kaiju's gut, then grabbed the gasping thug's arm. He raised the stunned man's arm, ducked under it and twisted to lock the elbow.

Kaiju hugged his battered abdomen and glanced up to see Trent hurl the henchman. Once again, one of the yakuza leader's own men crashed into him, knocking him to the floor. John Trent rushed to the desk and glanced about for the Nambu pistol discarded by the slain yakuza thug. He couldn't find the damn thing, so he moved behind Kaiju's desk and grabbed the *katana* from its stand.

Trent drew the sword from the scabbard. The three foot length of the ancient Japanese steel seemed to fill with slithering fire as light reflected along the polished blade. The weapon was magnificent, a work of art by a master swordsmith of the sixteenth century. Trent discarded the scabbard and grasped with both hands the long handle covered with sharkskin and twisted silk.

"There is a tradition that an *oyabun* of a yakuza should die by the sword," Trent remarked as he approached Kaiju. "Correct?"

"You can't kill me," Kaiju said, breathing heavily as he rose to his feet. "My ancestors formed the ninja clan that you are a member of. Your family ties with my family are centuries old. To take my life would be like killing your own blood kin."

"You're a disgrace to your ancestors, Kaiju," Trent replied as he moved closer, the *katana* extended before him, the tip of the blade held at eye level. "They will surely rest easier after you are dead...."

The door burst open, and two gun-wielding thugs attempted to muscle through the doorframe, crowding each other in their haste. Their clumsiness probably saved Trent's life. He immediately dashed forward and swung the *katana* in an overhead *shomen-uch* cut.

Flawless steel struck the closest gunman's arm. The sharp edge sliced through muscle and bone. The man screamed as his hand and half his forearm fell to the floor. A Nambu pistol was still clenched in the dismembered fist. Blood gushed from the abrupt amputation, and the hoodlum crumpled to his knees in a whimpering heap.

Trent barely glanced at the man he had maimed with the first sword stroke as he immediately thrust the *katana* into the chest of the second gunman. The steel tip pierced the yakuza stooge just under the breastbone, skewered his heart and punctured an exit near his left shoulder blade.

The thug gasped in horrified astonishment. A ribbon of blood trickled from his lips as his body convulsed around the sword blade that had been driven through it. Trent grabbed the man's wrist above the Government Issue 1911A1 Colt pistol in his fist. The American held the gun hand toward the ceiling as he pushed the *katana* handle with his other hand to force the dying man into the secretaries' office.

A bullet splintered wood from the doorway near Trent's head. The report of the gunshot came from within Kaiju's office. Either the *oyabun* or his surviving henchman inside had managed to get a gun. Trent shoved his lifeless victim into a secretary's desk as he ducked into the outer office and slammed the door with a hasty kick. Another bullet struck the walnut panels and penetrated wood.

"You really blew it, Trent," the American told himself as he plucked the .45 Colt from the dead man's grasp.

More bullets were fired through the door of Kaiju's office. One round pierced wood and tugged at the coattails of Trent's jacket. Excited voices shouted from the corridor beyond. More yakuza were coming to their *oyabun*'s rescue. If Trent remained in the secretaries' office, he would be boxed in and caught in a crossfire. At least in the corridor he had a fighting chance.

Trent left the *katana* in the dead man's body and headed for the hallway. Carefully he peered around the edge of the doorway. Two men dressed in dark blue uniforms with white leather gun belts dashed down the corridor toward the office. They were private security guards, not Tokyo police. Trent didn't know whether they were yakuza. Probably, he thought. Kaiju wouldn't trust his security to outsiders.

The American wanted to spare them if possible. Both guards carried Nambu pistols in their fists, the muzzles pointed toward the ceiling. Trent aimed his Colt high and fired a big .45 round above their heads.

The guards ducked. One man let go of his gun and the other dropped to a kneeling position and trained his Nambu on the doorway. Trent had little choice. He shot the guard in the face. A 230 grain bullet took out the back of the man's skull and splattered brain matter on the wall behind him.

The second security guard covered his head with his arms and begged for mercy in a chattering, sobbing voice. Trent jogged into the corridor and kicked the man's gun beyond easy reach and left him trembling in helpless fear.

The halls were empty. Trent glanced at the elevator. The light flashed on the "up" symbol. More reinforcements were on their way up, Trent concluded. He glanced around and found the fire escape stairs. Holding the Colt in his fist, he headed down the steps.

Shoe leather pounded the stairs below him, and he saw shadows dancing along the wall as two figures charged up the steps toward his position. Trent crouched by the railing post at the eighth-floor landing and waited for the adversaries to come into view.

One man with close-cropped hair was clearly a yakuza enforcer. He was dressed in an ill-fitting suit and wielded a pistol in one hand and a sword in the other. The latter weapon was crudely made with a blade shorter than a *katana* and longer than the *wakazashi*, the traditional short sword of a samurai.

It was roughly the same length as the *ninja-do* Trent favored, but the yakuza sword had a plain wooden handle without any hand guard at the quillon.

The other guy was another uniformed security guard. Trent promptly shot the yakuza thug in the center of the chest. The hood's sword and gun clattered on the stairs, and he tumbled backward. The security guard dropped to one knee and hastily fired his Nambu as Trent ducked behind the post.

The Japanese are notoriously bad shots with firearms, and the guard was no exception. His bullet ricocheted off the wall behind Trent. The American snap-aimed and fired his Colt. The guard sprawled down the stairs, nursing a bullet in his heart.

Trent sprinted down the steps and scooped up the Nambu dropped by the dead guard and the crude yakuza sword. Tucking the 9 mm pistol into his slacks at the small of his back, he concealed it with his jacket. He moved down to the sixth floor, the Colt in his right fist and the sword in his left.

Another yakuza thug met him on the fourth-floor landing. The hoodlum didn't appear to carry a gun, but held another cheapjack sword with a plain handle in his fists. Trent pointed his pistol at the muscular square-faced goon. The guy stiffened, swallowed hard and held his sword in an on-guard position.

"I'd probably shoot you," Trent remarked in English, speaking to himself more than to the Japanese thug, "but I don't want to make any more noise than I have to."

He thrust the Colt into his belt and gripped the sword with both hands as he descended slowly. The yakuza nodded with approval and rushed forward. He feinted an overhead cut to try to draw Trent's attention and quickly lunged his blade at the American's belly.

Trent was too good a swordsman to fall for such a trick. He blocked the lunge with his own blade and hooked a kick to the thug's right shoulder, knocking the guy off balance. Trent leaped down the last three risers, slashing his sword at his opponent while still in midair.

The American ninja landed on his feet and glanced over his shoulder at the yakuza swordsman. The thug was sprawled across the stairs with his sword still in his fist. A deep wound at the nape of his neck revealed where Trent's blade had severed the spinal cord.

At the second-story landing, Trent discovered a door to a loading ramp in an alley outside the building where some workmen were busy unpacking crates from a truck. None of the laborers seemed aware of what was going on inside the building. There were no police in the alley or the street beyond. Apparently Kaiju hadn't wanted to call in the law to deal with his problems. The yakuza tended to take care of their business without the police, a custom that suited Trent at the moment.

He wiped off the sword to get rid of fingerprints and left it inside the door. Trent buttoned his jacket to conceal the Colt pistol in his belt as he walked down the ramp. One of the workers smiled and waved, and

Trent returned the gesture and called *"ja mata"* to the men. He walked briskly from the alley and soon melted into the crowds in the streets of Tokyo.

"Well," he whispered to himself. "Guess I'll have to try something else now."

4

Ikeda Ken hadn't changed much since Phoenix Force first met him several years ago. The Kompei control officer was a small man of slight build who wore his hair parted in the middle. His horn-rimmed glasses rode low on his nose. Ikeda may have looked like a nerd, but he was a highly competent intelligence operative and a lot tougher than he appeared to be.

Ikeda had come to meet Phoenix Force at Tokyo International Airport. Arrangements had been made by the U.S. and Japanese governments to allow the five-man elite team to bypass customs inspections in order to bring weapons and other equipment into the country. The Kompei agent had been waiting at the runway when the TWA airliner landed. He made certain their crates and other luggage went directly into the back of the minibus brought for the occasion.

"Ikeda-san, ohayo gozaimasu," Katz greeted as he stepped from the plane's ramp and bowed to the Kompei officer. "I'm afraid that's about half the Japanese I've learned since we last met. I hope I pronounced your name right, at least."

"You did quite well, Katz-*san*," Ikeda replied, returning the bow. "It is a pleasure to see you again.

Although I must confess, I would be more comfortable if you had come to Japan as tourists this time."

"Maybe next time," Katz said with a smile.

"At least your arrival is somewhat less exciting than the first time you were at this airport," Ikeda remarked.

"What happened the first time?" Calvin James inquired.

"You remember what happened when we arrived in Istanbul?" Rafael Encizo asked as he and James approached Ikeda.

"Who could forget?" James answered. "Damn terrorists tried to kill us as soon as we stepped off the bloody plane."

"That's what happened the first time we were in Tokyo, too," Encizo explained. "So far, things are going pretty smooth, huh?"

"We're not out of the airport yet," Gary Manning commented. He turned to Ikeda and bowed. *"Ikeda-san, ogenki desuka?"*

"I am fine, thank you," Ikeda replied. "Your accent is better than I recall, Gary-*san*. Has Keio taught you more Japanese? I do not see him with your group. I hope he is not ill."

"Keio has been dead for almost four years," Katz told him, a trace of sorrow still creeping into his voice despite the passing of time since Ohara's death.

"I . . . I am sorry," Ikeda said, shaking his head. "I knew he was no longer in Japan, but I assumed he was living in the United States. This is sad news."

"If it's any comfort to you, Ikeda-*san*," McCarter commented as he nodded a greeting to the Kompei agent, "Keio died bravely on the battlefield. I think that was how he wanted to die. Certainly the way *I* want to go when my time comes. I just hope I can do it as well as Keio did."

"That's a great comfort," Ikeda said lamely. He didn't find the idea of being killed in combat the least bit desirable, but Ikeda recalled that all five warriors had seemed a little crazy. Except the Englishman. He seemed to be very crazy, in Ikeda's opinion.

"We've got a new friend here," Encizo stated. "Ikeda Ken, meet Calvin James."

"Feels funny to be introduced to somebody using my real name for a change," James said, bowing to the Asian. "Pleasure to meet you, Ikeda-*san*."

"The pleasure is mine," the Kompei man assured him. "Is this your first time in Japan, James-*san*?"

"No," James answered. "I spent liberty here a couple times while I was in the Navy. I was wounded in Vietnam and spent a couple months in a hospital in Okinawa and got to spend a few extra weekends in Tokyo. Great city. Especially compared to Saigon."

"Welcome back," Ikeda said with another bow. "Now, shall we board the bus and discuss business in a more private setting?"

Phoenix Force agreed. The idle chitchat and formal greeting and introductions seemed a bit absurd to Westerners, but it was an essential part of *enryo*, the Japanese code of proper conduct that emphasizes reserve and constraint. That is a highly respected part of the Japanese culture. Emotions are controlled, dangerous tasks are discussed in a calm way, accomplishments are referred to in a modest manner. Boasting is annoying and not acceptable. Complaining or negative input is also a social taboo.

The attitudes cultivated by *enryo* have always had a great influence on the Japanese people and their culture. They may account, to some degree, for their polite and generally law-abiding society. *Enryo* may have contributed to Japan's economic success since World War II.

Despite Ikeda's remark about discussing business as if he wished to assault the problem directly, he still exchanged more social niceties as the bus rolled onto Namiki Dori and headed for downtown Tokyo. The men of Phoenix Force were patient and polite. That is the only way to get cooperation from a typical Japanese.

Calvin James wished John Trent was with them. The American ninja understood the behavior of the Japanese. Trent's personality was probably influenced more by his Japanese upbringing than by his later life in America. Yet Trent had always claimed there was no great difference between the people of his mother's nation and Americans.

He gazed out a window, allowing the others to chat with Ikeda. Tokyo looked much the same as it had when James had visited the city as a sailor on liberty almost fifteen years ago. Incredible, he thought. Was Vietnam really that long ago? Sometimes it seemed as

though he had just left the jungles yesterday, and
sometimes it seemed a hundred years ago.

Tokyo seemed to have even more modern buildings
and skyscrapers than James recalled. It was a modern
city in every sense of the term, with all the advantages
and evils that go with the title. Tokyo had monorails
and bullet trains, but it also had acute housing problems and monstrous traffic jams. An incredible assortment of stores, restaurants, businesses and
entertainment centers offered variety, but the city
suffered from pollution and the collective strain of
people living at a very hectic pace.

Besides its modernity, Tokyo was also an ancient
city. The Imperial Palace was visible among the spaces
between towers of concrete and steel in the distance.
It was a reminder of the centuries-old culture and history of Japan that, according to legend, dates back to
660 B.C. Japan had seen many changes during those
long centuries. The country had been ruled by emperors and fierce shogun warlords. Japan successfully
fought a naval war with Russia at the turn of the century and later joined with the Axis powers to challenge the rest of the world during World War II.

Japan had been defeated but recovered dramati-
cally after the war. One of the most bitter enemies of
the United States and the Western democracies had
become a great ally and a champion of capitalism and
free enterprise.

Evidence of that was everywhere in signs bearing
legends written in English as well as Japanese ideographs. The Sony building resembled the United Na-

tions headquarters and was nearly as large. The Sanyo building was also located in the Ginza section, well-known for its exciting nightlife and popular restaurants. Branches of numerous American corporations, ranging from Chase Manhattan Bank to Pepsi-Cola, were as notable in Tokyo as the Japanese products popular in the U.S. cities.

That served to remind the men of Phoenix Force that the United States and Japan had close economic and political ties. It was important to keep relations between the two nations in good condition. If Trent was a yakuza hit man, he threatened to upset that equilibrium, as well as jeopardize the security of Phoenix Force and Stony Man.

PHOENIX FORCE DIDN'T GET AROUND to discussing the mission with Ikeda Ken until they gathered in the Kompei agent's office on Annex Avenue. The enormous Matsuzakaya Department was located on the corner of Annex and Ginza, so the area was always filled with activity and a lot of people. No one paid much attention to the minibus or its passengers. They left the vehicle and entered a small nondescript office building.

"A most curious situation," Ikeda remarked, sipping tea as he listened to Phoenix Force explain their reason for being in Japan. He was certain they had left out a few details, but that was to be expected. "An American coming to Japan to carry out ninja assassinations is certainly an ironic reversal of what one would ordinarily expect."

"We don't know John is responsible," James insisted. "He could be innocent, but we gotta check it out."

"You called Trent 'John,' James-*san*," Ikeda noticed. "And your manner is almost defensive. Do you know this man well?"

"We've worked with him before," Katz confessed somewhat reluctantly. "He assisted us on three missions."

"So?" The Kompei agent raised his scant eyebrows. "Then this Trent must be a very dangerous and resourceful man. Are you certain he is not a double agent? Possibly working for the Soviet KGB?"

"Very unlikely," Gary Manning replied, wishing Ikeda had offered coffee instead of Japanese green tea. "The yakuza connection is far more likely. Trent's uncle is a subchief of the American branch of the Kaiju Clan."

"Kaiju?" Ikeda nodded his head, a gesture that can mean many different things in Japan. A nod can mean anything from "yes" or "I agree" to "get the hell away from me."

"Is the Kaiju Clan something special?" Rafael Encizo inquired as he helped David McCarter start to open their crates.

"Perhaps," Ikeda replied. "The Kaiju yakuza are lead by Kaiju Hideo, supposedly a direct descendant of the founders of the clan. Interesting history. The Kaiju were originally a ninja clan. Your Trent may be working for this *oyabun*. Yes?"

"Possibly," Katz agreed, lighting a Camel cigarette with his battered old Ronson lighter. "I'm curious, Ikeda-*san*. There are hundreds of yakuza clans operating in Japan. Why are you so familiar with the Kaiju?"

"Because Kaiju Hideo is the president of a legitimate import-export business," Ikeda began. A common Japanese trait is an unwillingness to address a subject directly, and Ikeda was very Japanese in this respect. "Many *oyabun* run legal businesses here. Well, earlier this morning, there was a very violent incident at Kaiju's office building. Seven of his men were killed. Some were shot to death. Others died by sword. Kaiju himself did not call the police, but one of his employees did. No doubt, it was someone who failed to realize the *oyabun* would rather keep such things from the eyes of the authorities."

"That is interesting," Katz stated. "What did Kaiju tell the Tokyo police?"

"He claimed a band of leftist fanatics burst into his office and tried to kill him because he's a capitalist oppressor of the masses," Ikeda laughed. "Good story, yes? Communist troublemakers assault a hardworking businessman. That would make Kaiju an honorable man to many here in Japan."

"But you don't believe this story?" Manning asked.

"Certainly not," Ikeda confirmed. "The killings are most probably the work of a rival yakuza gang. A rather clumsy assault. Probably a small clan."

"I'd think gang warfare would cause more concern," Manning remarked. "Yakuza wars can be nasty. There was a real bloodbath going on a couple years ago.''

"Hai," Ikeda agreed. "The worse yakuza war was in 1959. Entire clans were wiped out. Many men killed. No one knows how many. But, frankly, the gangsters kill other gangsters and rarely harm civilians. No one gets too upset by yakuza killing yakuza. The big *oyabun* are seldom attacked, and they are usually powerful and influential men in society. Very difficult to arrest. Difficult to kill.''

"How does the Kaiju rank among the yakuza clans?" James inquired. "Big fish or little fish?"

"Bigger than *koi*, smaller than sharks," Ikeda answered. "The Kaiju Clan are medium or average in power. Certainly not equal to the big clans like the Midori-eero Tora or the Hebe Uji."

James exclaimed with surprise, "Isn't the Hebe Uji the Snake Clan?"

"That is correct," the Kompei man confirmed. "They have grown quite rapidly over the last few years. No one is quite certain why they have been so successful. Are you familiar with this yakuza clan?"

"Damn right," Manning stated. "The Snake Clan is part of TRIO. Ever hear of it?"

"No," Ikeda admitted. "Are they terrorists?"

"TRIO is a worldwide criminal syndicate," Katz explained. "It's a combine of three large Asian criminal societies—the Chinese Black Serpent Tong, a Mongolian outfit that calls itself the New Horde and the Snake Clan yakuza. It's one of the most dangerous international hoodlum outfits in the world, and one of the least known.''

"Chinese and Mongols working with Japanese yakuza?'' Ikeda frowned. "Most unusual.''

"But true,'' Manning assured him. "We've encountered TRIO on more than one occasion. They're for real.''

"Say,'' David McCarter began as he buckled a shoulder-holster rig around his upper back and shoved a 9 mm Browning Hi-Power auto pistol into leather. "What can you tell us about this Nagano bloke who was murdered two days ago? That's the one that might be Trent's handiwork.''

"He was a well-placed yakuza representative of the Midori-eero Tora,'' Ikeda answered. "The Green Tiger Clan, one of the largest yakuza gangs in Tokyo and Kyoto. However, he was probably of minimal importance to them. Probably the Tigers had him killed for some offense which we may never know about.''

"How do you know he wasn't important?'' Encizo asked, checking the cocking knob of his Heckler and Koch MP-5 machine pistol.

"Because Nagano hired private security for bodyguards,'' Ikeda explained. "If he was important, the Tigers would have supplied him with yakuza bodyguards.''

"Shit,'' James muttered as he approached the crates to remove a Jackass Leather rig from the box. He slid into the shoulder holster and slid a .45 caliber Colt Commander into the leather scabbard under his left arm and clipped a Jet-Aer dagger with sheath under his right. "Why the hell was he killed?"

"When we know that," Katz mused, "we'll have a pretty good idea *who* did it, as well."

5

Phoenix Force had two possible leads to check out. One was the Kin-Rakooda Automobile Corporation that Nagano Jiro had belonged to and the other was the Yoee-Uma Import-Export Company where Kaiju Hideo had claimed that leftist radicals killed seven of his employees. The two incidents could be totally unconnected, but the murder of Nagano had led to Phoenix Force's current mission to find Trent, and the Kaiju Clan was the same yakuza outfit Trent's uncle belonged to.

The team split up. Calvin James, David McCarter and Rafael Encizo headed for the Kin-Rakooda Corporation. Yakov Katzenelenbogen, Gary Manning and Ikeda Ken would meet with Kaiju at the Yoee-Uma building. Since Kaiju was known to be the leader of a yakuza clan, Ikeda had decided to accompany Katz and Manning. Kaiju wouldn't dare start any trouble with an official from Kompei present. At least, that was the theory.

A receptionist in the lobby of the Yoee-Uma headquarters called Kaiju and told the company president that three men wanted to see him—a Kompei officer and two special investigators from Interpol. Kaiju put her on hold for half a minute and then informed her to send the gentlemen up to the eighth floor.

Kaiju Hideo personally met the trio at the elevators. The *oyabun*'s toad face managed a sickly imitation of a smile as he greeted the visitors. They exchanged formal bows and handshakes. Katz and Manning noticed that Kaiju didn't like shaking hands and did so as quickly as possible to get the unpleasant chore out of the way.

"I understand you speak English, Mr. Kaiju," Ikeda began. "If we may use that language, it will help save time in conversation. Mr. Brennan and Mr. Colby do not speak Japanese, and I would have to translate if you decline to speak in English."

"I have no wish to cause difficulties, Ikeda-*san*," Kaiju assured the Kompei agent. "I will be happy to answer any questions, but I do not understand why Interpol is interested in what happened here this morning."

Kaiju's English was quite good, other than a little problem in pronouncing words with the letter *l* in them.

"We have reason to believe the men who attacked your building may have been part of an international band of criminals who are wanted in several other countries," Katz replied. The Phoenix Force linguist spoke English with a nondescript accent that confused people who tried to put a label on it. It wasn't quite British, yet it didn't have any definite midwestern American or New England quality.

"You suspect the Japanese Red Army?" Kaiju smiled. "I think not, gentlemen. They were student radicals. Most probably advocates of a Marxist college professor who should be expelled from our country for stirring up such rabble."

"We don't think the Japanese Red Army is involved," Gary Manning assured him. "The JRA is practically extinct. The borderline members—the majority of the JRA—left the outfit when it became more violent back in the early seventies. A lot of the fanatics that remained were either killed by police or committed suicide. Virtually all the surviving JRA members are no longer in Japan. It's believed there are only about forty or fifty of them left. Most of them are probably living in terrorist training camps in South Yemen."

"I am pleased to see Interpol has taken such interest in international terrorism," Kaiju declared. "Those mad dogs are a threat to all decent people throughout the entire world. Do you wish to see my office? It is on the tenth floor. The police have it blocked off. They are still examining the room for fingerprints and other things that I am sure you know more about than I."

"We don't need to see your office," Katz assured him. The Phoenix Force pair had no desire to encounter curious Tokyo police who might question the identities of the "Interpol agents." "However, we would like to speak with you privately, Mister Kaiju."

"Of course," the oyabun agreed. "I have a temporary office set up on this floor. Follow me, please."

Kaiju escorted them to his new office. It was almost as big as his presidential office on the tenth floor. He had an oak desk, brown leather furniture and a wet bar with a large mirror behind it. Kaiju walked to the bar and removed balloon glasses from a rack.

"I have some fine French brandy," he announced. "Seventy years old. Will you join me, or are you forbidden alcohol because you are on duty?"

"None for me, thank you," Ikeda stated.

"Little early for me," Manning remarked. "Thanks, anyway."

"It is for me, too," Katz stated. "But seventy-year-old brandy is a rare opportunity. I would like a glass, Kaiju-*san*."

"My pleasure," Kaiju assured him, pouring liquor into two glasses. "Now, perhaps you can tell me what this is about?"

"Of course," Katz said, accepting a glass of brandy. "Do you know of an international band of cutthroats by the name of TRIO?"

Kaiju stared at the Phoenix Force commander as if he had just told the *oyabun* that both his parents had been killed by hostile aliens from Mars. Kaiju quickly raised his glass and gulped some brandy before he spoke.

"I think you refer to the Triad," Kaiju remarked. "Chinese tong, involved in heroin and other criminal activity. Yes?"

"TRIO is entirely different," Katz explained, "although a Chinese tong society is associated with TRIO. The Black Serpent Tong, not the Triad."

"I don't think these criminals would be interested in me or my business," Kaiju remarked as he moved to his desk.

"There's also a yakuza clan connected with TRIO," Manning added. "The Snake Clan. I understand they're fairly active in Tokyo. Surely you've heard of them."

"I am a respectable businessman," Kaiju declared, seated behind his desk with the chair pulled in close. He held the brandy glass in his left hand while his right slid under the desk. "I know nothing about yakuza."

"Or TRIO?" Katz asked with a smile.

"I never heard of it before you spoke of this matter," Kaiju declared, gulping more brandy. "And if you are making any accusations, I wish to call my lawyer."

"This is good brandy," Katz remarked, sipping some liquid from his glass. "You shouldn't gulp it, Mr. Kaiju."

"We are not accusing you of anything, Kaiju-*san*," Ikeda assured him. "But we are curious about this wild band of leftist students you reported. You have security guards, trained and licensed to carry firearms, yet they failed to stop these 'students.' Indeed, two of them were killed. None of them even succeeded in wounding any of the invaders. These wild-eyed radicals must have been remarkably lucky, since one would assume they were relatively unskilled."

"They caught us off guard," Kaiju replied. "My security was not adequate. After all, I did not expect to be a victim of such terrorism."

"Were they all Japanese?" Manning asked. "Is it possible one of them may have been a Eurasian? Maybe part Japanese and part Caucasian?"

Kaiju bit his lip. He swallowed the rest of his brandy. Kaiju held the glass in front of his face for a moment and placed it on the desk.

"I don't think so," he declared. "Why do you ask?"

"Because we're looking for a man named John Trent," Katz said in a flat, hard voice. "He knows who we are. Give him a description of us."

The Israeli pulled a pearl-gray glove from his right hand to reveal the extremity made of steel with metal cables extending along the back of the artificial fingers and wrist. He held the back of the "hand" toward Kaiju, pointing the hollow tip of the index finger toward the ceiling.

"This will make it easier to describe us," the Israeli stated. "And he damn well better talk to us, or there's going to be a lot of heat on a certain *oyabun* of a certain yakuza clan that bears his name."

"I think I shall call my lawyer now," Kaiju said, reaching for the phone on his desk.

"Gee," Manning commented. "You mean that isn't who you signaled to when you pushed that button under your desk? Or did you just do that to call your secretary in to take notes? Better have a talk with her. She's pretty slow. Taking her a long time to get in here. Maybe she's waiting out in the hall."

"No one is waiting in the hall," Kaiju said, his hand resting on the telephone. "But I can have security remove you from my property, and I warn you that I have powerful friends in government who can cause even Kompei reason for concern. Your organization was not created to harass Japanese citizens, Ikeda-*san.*"

"We're leaving, Kaiju-*san,*" Ikeda assured him. "But we may return to ask more questions."

"I have not known the answers to any you have asked this day," Kaiju snapped. "I have been a victim of lunatics with guns and swords, but you dare to treat me as a criminal. If you cause me further trouble, I shall have my lawyers and friends in government deal with you. Good day, gentlemen!"

"Thanks for the brandy," Katz said, placing his glass on the bar. He stared into the mirror for a moment. "We'd better leave now."

THE VISIT WASN'T DISCUSSED by Katzenelenbogen, Manning and Ikeda until they were inside the Kompei agent's Toyota. Ikeda steered the vehicle into the street, and they were soon in the middle of another unavoidable Tokyo traffic jam.

"I had not expected you to question Kaiju about TRIO or confront him so directly about Trent," Ikeda remarked. "What did you hope to accomplish?"

"I wanted to see how Kaiju would react," Katz explained. "And he certainly knew about both TRIO and Trent. Kaiju-*san* isn't a great actor, but he thinks fast and he kept his head. The man isn't going to break down and give us any solid evidence just by chatting with him. But he still gave away enough."

"But why are you curious about TRIO?" Ikeda asked.

"'Cause they're enemies," Manning answered. "If they're active in Japan and find out we're here, they may just try to take us out of the picture. We've screwed up some of their plans before. TRIO is a sore loser."

"And TRIO could be connected with the Nagano murder or the incident at Kaiju's office," Katz added. "I just hope Trent isn't working for TRIO. He knows who we are and how we operate."

"And he's dangerous," Manning commented. "I'm not sure any of us could take him without a gun, especially if Trent has his ninja weapons."

"Well, when we find him we'd better have our guns ready," Katz said with a shrug. "And Kaiju might just send him to us."

"I doubt that," Ikeda said with a frown as he steered the car around a Honda motorcycle that had broken down in the street. "More likely, Kaiju will tell Trent to go into hiding or flee the country."

"Trent is already in hiding," Manning stated. "Or at least nobody knows where he is. Trent arrived at Tokyo Airport two weeks ago, and that's all anybody knows. Where he's been and what he's been doing is anybody's guess, but there's evidence he killed Nagano."

"He's a suspect," Katz reminded him. "We don't know anything for sure, and we don't want to gun down Trent on sight and later find out he was innocent."

"You've just warned Kaiju that you're looking for Trent," Ikeda insisted. "He will be harder than ever to find."

"If he's working for Kaiju, the *oyabun*'s first concern will be with his clan and the success of his business," Katz replied. "I don't think Kaiju is the sort to jeopardize that to protect Trent. The guy's a bastard, and I suspect he doesn't like Americans much. He may have Trent killed and dumped on the doorstep of Kompei headquarters...or try. Trent isn't an easy man to kill."

"I thought you did not want Trent harmed," Ikeda remarked.

"Not if he's innocent," Katz confirmed. "And if he's innocent, he isn't working for Kaiju. If he's become a yakuza hit man, I'd rather have Kaiju kill him than be forced to do it myself."

"Katz-*san*—" Ikeda glanced at the Phoenix Force commander with a startled expression "—you speak of murder."

"Realistically," Katz said with a sigh. "If Trent is working for the other side, we'll probably have to kill him. I don't think he'll want to go to prison. He'll probably force us to kill him before allowing that to happen."

"Might even kill himself," Manning mused. "You know, it seemed to me that Kaiju didn't just recognize Trent's name. I got the impression he might be scared of Trent."

"Maybe he's got reason to be," Katz commented. "It occurred to me that Kaiju's men were shot and killed by sword. Trent could have done it."

"You think he could have killed seven men?" Ikeda asked. "They were armed security guards and probably *kobun*—yakuza enforcers who often carry guns, although most are far better with knife or sword."

"They'd have to be *very* good to be a match for Trent," Katz stated. "He could have done it, but that's wishful thinking. Trent is probably working with Kaiju or some related yakuza clan. He helped assassinate Nagano and the Green Tigers...the yakuza clan that Nagano was connected with, right?"

"Hai," Ikeda said with a nod, bringing the Toyota to a halt at a stoplight. "The Green Tiger Clan."

"Yeah," Katz continued. "They probably hit Kaiju today as retaliation for Nagano's murder. Which means we've arrived in Tokyo just in time for a yakuza gang war, and we're right in the middle of it, looking for a man who can turn himself into a shadow."

Another car skidded to a halt behind the Toyota. It bumped into the rear of Ikeda's car, jarring the occupants. Katz and Manning automatically reached for the pistols under their jackets, but the driver of the second vehicle was already shouting apologies as he stepped from his car and tried to unlock the fenders.

"Chikusho!" Ikeda rasped as he started to get out of the car to inspect the damage.

"What did you say?" Manning asked, also stepping from the Toyota.

"It is an expression I would rather not translate," Ikeda replied with a trace of embarrassment in his voice.

KAIJU HIDEO SAT behind the desk, sipping more brandy. The knock at his door didn't surprise him. He told the visitor to enter, well aware who must be on the other side of the door.

Matsuno Sadatoshi entered the office. A tall man, Matsuno was lean with sculptured muscles and a face as hard as granite. He wore a black suit with a matching shirt, open at the neck. Matsuno carried a *katana* in his left hand, the silver and sharkskin handle tilted near his belt buckle, within reach of his right hand for a lightning-fast *iai* draw.

Matsuno wasn't threatening Kaiju. He always carried the samurai sword of his family and would sooner surrender his own life than give up his *katana*. Matsuno believed, like the samurai warriors of the past, that the sword is the soul of a soldier. Without it, he is nothing.

"Did you see them, Matsuno-*san*?" Kaiju inquired, although he already knew the answer. "You heard our conversation?"

"*Hai,*" the tall man replied with a nod.

Matsuno had received the signal to enter the room next to Kaiju's new office when the *oyabun* had pressed the button under his desk. He had watched Katz, Manning and Ikeda through the one-way glass of the mirror over the bar.

"Then you know Interpol has taken an interest in TRIO," Kaiju remarked, drinking the brandy with nervous gulps.

"Those men were not Interpol," Matsuno stated, his eyes black flames of controlled anger. "I recognize them. They are our worst enemies. I saw them in the Philippines more than two years ago. They and three companions crushed a major TRIO operation at the time. Only I survived and escaped when those five devils attacked the boat we were using as a floating base. I have prayed to the gods and my ancestors that one day I would have revenge. Now, my karma has delivered the enemies to me. Their blood shall be spilled to wash away the burden of my obligation to the souls of my slain comrades."

"I understand," Kaiju began slowly, choosing his words with care. Matsuno was an extremely dangerous man. A fanatic who would not hesitate to kill if he felt offended. "But I ask you not to permit emotion to override reason. We have other problems, Matsuno-*san*...."

"The Kaiju Clan is now part of the Snake Clan," Matsuno declared. "That means you are also now with TRIO. If you do not care to continue that arrangement, say so now. Of course, if you are not with TRIO, you are against us. You know how we deal with enemies, Kaiju-*san*."

"I do not wish to change our arrangement," Kaiju assured him, wishing he had more brandy in his glass. "However, I must remind you that we have urgent business to deal with. The expansion of my clan to meet the new demands of TRIO. The problems we can expect from the Green Tiger Clan, and I may also be forced to deal with that half-breed lunatic Trent."

"The five foreigners remain our greatest threat," Matsuno insisted. "The Green Tiger Clan is no match for us, especially after the other clans decide to join TRIO. And they will either join us, or we'll destroy them. Any *oyabun* who refuses shall die, and any of his *kobun* who intend to free-lance shall be turned into examples for others. Examples so terrible that no one will dare to oppose us. TRIO has some Chinese and Mongols who specialize in such work."

Matsuno spoke of Chinese and Mongols as if they were loathsome animal life, several notches beneath human beings. He felt that the Japanese were intellectually and culturally superior to other Asians—and non-Asians were on an even lower level. Matsuno considered Europeans to be whimpering daydreamers who cling to the past because their future is abysmal. He believed the Russians were uncouth brutes and tactless liars. The Americans had brought advanced technology to Japan and other nations, but they had lost their spirit due to weak living and slothful habits.

"What of Trent?" Kaiju asked lamely.

"You think a half-breed American with a whore mother and a cowardly uncle is a genuine threat?" Matsuno shook his head. "I begin to wonder if you are the sort of man TRIO needs, Kaiju-*san*."

"I also underestimated Trent," Kaiju stated. "You would not take him so lightly if you had been here this morning."

"If I had been here this morning," Matsuno replied smugly, "I would have killed that piece of toad slime. But, no matter. Trent is not a problem for TRIO. In fact, I don't think he's really a problem for anyone now. He was lucky enough to escape with his life. He's an American. That means he values his life more than honor or family or obligations to any cause. Trent is probably headed back to America by now."

"I'm not so sure," Kaiju admitted. "But Trent is my concern, not yours or TRIO's. However, I suggest the decision of priorities be made by our superiors, Shimo Goro and the other two leaders of TRIO. *Hai?*"

"Their decision shall be exactly what I have told you," Matsuno declared. "Now, I want you to contact your *kobun* who are scattered about the city. Especially those among the workers at the Kin-Rakooda Automobile Corporation."

"Why there?" Kaiju asked, already reaching for the phone.

"Because those two bastards were asking about TRIO and about Trent," Matsuno explained. "Trent is an American, and one of the idiots who accompanied me the night we assassinated Nagano is also an American of Japanese descent. The fool left an American-made *tanto* knife in the chest of one of Nagano's bodyguards. I think our enemies suspect Trent did this. For some reason, they're interested in the Nagano killing."

"And you think they'll go to the Kin-Rakooda Corporation?" Kaiju asked, doubting the other man's logic.

"I think it is quite possible," Matsuno confirmed. "Now contact your men, and I'll describe those five murderous scum in detail. I memorized their faces. I've been seeing those faces over and over again for two and half years."

"I'm certain you'll give a good description," Kaiju said with a sigh. "But what do you want my *kobun* to do if they find these men?"

"That should be obvious," Matsuno replied. "Order your men to kill them. They are to kill the enemy on sight."

6

"This was a bloody waste of time," David McCarter complained as he stepped from the office of the president of the Kin-Rakooda Automobile Corporation. "If that bloke knows anything about Nagano's connection with the yakuza, he's not going to admit it because it's the same as admitting he's got connections himself."

"Let's talk about this after we leave the building," Rafael Encizo urged as he and Calvin James followed McCarter into the corridor. "Not the sort of thing we want everybody in the place to listen in on."

"Yeah," James added. "We might as well talk about the weather or something, anyway. This notion sure drew a blank."

The three Phoenix Force commandos had spent half an hour with the president of the auto corporation. They spoke with the executive through an interpreter, discussing Nagano Jiro's death and a possible yakuza connection. The company president stated that he had noticed some changes in Nagano's personality. The vice president had seemed strangely broody and paranoid the week before his death. However, the head of Kin-Rakooda had claimed he knew nothing about any yakuza dealings involving either Nagano or the company.

The Phoenix Force trio had left the office disappointed but not surprised that their efforts had failed to produce results. It had been a long shot at best, but they had few leads and had to check into anything and everything that might help them find Trent or learn if the American ninja had been involved in Nagano's murder.

They walked by a set of large picture windows overlooking the factory below. Workers were busily assembling engine blocks and building the skeletal framework of automobiles. Others were attaching seats and upholstery while some laborers lowered shell-like outer car bodies into place.

Main shafts, axles, gears and electrical wiring were being installed. Tires were put into place, and car bodies were sanded and painted at the end of the assembly lines. More than two hundred workers were visible from the windows, which showed only a small portion of the plant. The laborers were clad in orange coveralls, yellow safety helmets, goggles and ear protectors. Few of them glanced up or looked around while they worked. Conversation seemed minimal, yet the laborers appeared to be in fairly good spirits as they worked.

The workers displayed greater enthusiasm for their labor than most Americans employed as assembly-line personnel. Maybe Japanese companies are run differently, Calvin James thought as he stared down at the line workers. Or maybe the Japanese simply regard their jobs differently than most Americans working in similar occupations. Perhaps the Japanese are more enthusiastic because steel mills and factories are not shutting down in Japan as they are in much of the American Midwest. Maybe they have more reason to believe they will still have jobs next year. That can certainly influence one's attitude, the black American concluded.

The workplace at the Kin-Rakooda plant seemed cleaner and better organized than the factory assembly lines James had seen as a kid in Chicago. The golden camel symbol of the Kin-Rakooda auto company was mounted on a wall above the assembly line, as well as several signs written in ideographs that James figured were probably slogans and safety reminders.

"Considering a new occupation in case we get fired?" McCarter asked, noticing James's interest in the auto workers. "Might not be a bad idea if we don't make some progress in this bloody mission. What the hell are we doing playing detective in bleedin' Tokyo?"

"Not our usual kind of mission," Encizo agreed with a shrug. "Okay with me if we don't get any more like it."

"Yeah," James agreed. "I don't like this crap about hunting down a friend as if he's a mad dog."

"Well," McCarter said with a yawn. "So far we haven't got a clue where to start looking for Trent."

"Hell, David." Encizo chuckled. "We've only been in Japan for five hours. What do you expect? Instant success? Maybe you should attend one of those real-estate seminars.''

"I might as well," the Briton complained as he took a pack of Players from his pocket. "It would be about as exciting as this assignment has been—"

Five sinister figures suddenly appeared at the head of the stairs at the end of the hallway. They wore orange coveralls and helmets like the assembly-line personnel below, but their faces were covered by black scarf masks. Three of them drew large *tanto* knives with nine-inch blades. Another man held a silencer-equipped pistol while the fifth man gripped a *waka-zashi* sword in both hands.

"Happy now?" James growled at McCarter as the armed gang charged.

They attacked swiftly, closing in before the three Phoenix fighters could draw their guns from shoulder leather. The attack was smoothly launched with the swordsman in the lead, the three knife artists following close behind and the gunman positioned at the rear.

The strategy was simple and logical. The guys with the blades intended to take out the Phoenix Force members. Knives and swords kill more quietly than guns—even a silenced pistol. A knife cut or a sword thrust cannot be traced by ballistics. The weapons had been made in a makeshift armory, the blades of cheap but razor-sharp steel, with simple wooden handles. The gunman held a 7.65 mm automatic imported from the Hong Kong black market. The gun was as untraceable as the sword and knife, but the gunman wouldn't use his weapon unless his comrades were in trouble.

The swordsman raised his *wakazashi* in a *shomen-uch* overhead cut as he charged toward Encizo. The Cuban didn't retreat, stepping instead toward his attacker and thrusting the heel of his left palm into the butt of the sword before his opponent could complete the stroke. Encizo locked his elbow and braced his right leg to form a solid barrier to restrain the swordsman.

Encizo's right hand slid under his jacket to the small of his back, and he swiftly drew his Cold Steel Tanto from its leather scabbard. The American-made version of the centuries-old samurai knife streaked forward in a rapid underhand thrust. Six inches of high-quality steel from Ventura, California, plunged into the swordsman's chest. The man screamed as Encizo shoved the blade into the aggressor's heart.

Blood splashed Encizo's wrist. More crimson liquid spilled from the dying man's lips. Encizo barely noticed. He was too busy holding back the killer's sword and turning the Tanto blade in his opponent's flesh. That increased the damage of the wound and helped Encizo work the knife free.

A knife-wielding opponent attacked David McCarter, holding his blade high in an overhand grip. A surprisingly amateurish attack, it almost worked because McCarter thought it must be a feint until the knife descended toward his face.

However, McCarter's lightning-quick reflexes dealt with the situation. He seized the wrist behind the knife with one hand and grabbed the guy's coverall front with his other. The Briton pulled, increasing his opponent's forward momentum. McCarter dropped back on a hip and a buttock and raised a foot. He landed on his back, pulled harder and thrust his boot into the attacker's abdomen.

McCarter straightened his knee and sent the Japanese hoodlum sailing overhead in a judo "circle throw." The man crashed to the floor without ceremony. McCarter rolled onto all fours and scrambled toward his dazed opponent. The knifeman started to rise, but McCarter kicked him in the ribs and quickly grabbed the thug's arm before he could use the knife.

The Briton chopped the side of his left hand into the crook of his opponent's elbow. The Asian's arm bent from the *shuto* stroke, and McCarter gripped the man's fist holding the knife and pushed the *tanto* into its owner. The blade pierced the hood's throat. Sharp steel severed the carotid and jugular before cutting a bloody path through the side of the goon's neck. The man's scarf mask was splashed with crimson as he slumped to the floor in a dying spasm.

Calvin James had met the charge of another attacker who lunged at the black commando's belly with a *tanto* poised in an underhand position. James agilely dodged the thrust and swung a sword-foot kick to the knife artist's wrist. The *tanto* hurled from the thug's hand.

James snapped a fast back-fist stroke to the side of his opponent's head. The guy grunted and stumbled into a wall but managed to throw a snap kick to

James's abdomen. The black warrior doubled up with a gasp. A shape suddenly filled his vision, and something whirled just above his head, brushing his hair.

Ironically, the guy who kicked James in the gut had unintentionally saved his life. The third knife artist had attacked and slashed a vicious *tanto* swipe at James's throat, but the Phoenix fighter had ducked beneath the attack.

He quickly pumped both fists into the second attacker's torso. The double punch hit the man in the stomach and chest, driving him backward four feet. James followed him and leaped forward to deliver a flying kick to the Asian thug's face. The tae kwon-do kick broke the guy's jawbone and knocked him out cold.

James's first opponent attacked him from behind, swinging a karate chop at the black tough guy's neck. The Phoenix pro had already started to turn to face the enemy and saw the attack in time to block the *shuto* stroke with a shoulder. A sharp pain stabbed at the ulnar nerve at the top of his shoulder, but James ignored it and swung a left hook to his opponent's jaw.

The thug's head danced from the punch. But he was tough, and suddenly lunged forward, hands extended, fingers rigid in vertical spear-hand thrusts. James dodged the deadly attack and grabbed one of the man's arms. The Phoenix pro yanked hard to use his opponent's own weight and movement against him—a fundamental principle of jujitsu. Then James turned sharply, locking the hood's arm at the wrist and elbow.

He released his opponent and hurled the man headfirst into a wall. Too late, James realized that "the wall" against which he had thrown the thug was actually a picture window. The Asian screamed as he crashed through the wide glass pane. Broken glass shards sliced half a dozen wounds in the unlucky man's flesh, but that was likely to be a lesser concern as he plunged six meters to the hard concrete floor of the assembly shop below.

Alarmed voices cried out as the body fell and connected with the merciless surface with an ugly smack and a crunch of breaking bone. Workers rushed about in all directions. Some stared up at the windows and pointed at the three Phoenix Force commandos and the last attacker who was trying to pick his target.

The gunman hesitated too long. Rafael Encizo suddenly hurled his Cold Steel Tanto at the hood, and David McCarter had drawn his Browning Hi-Power, snap-aimed and triggered the weapon. The big knife struck the thug in the center of the chest. The heavy blade split the breastbone and drove sternal shards into the man's heart and lungs. A 9 mm parabellum slug from McCarter's pistol punched through the guy's rib cage and drilled a destructive tunnel into his heart. The man was twice dead before he fell to the floor.

"What the hell was that about?" McCarter wondered aloud as he returned his Browning to shoulder leather.

"I think some guys just tried to kill us," James answered, rubbing his sore shoulder.

"Sure seemed like it," Encizo agreed as he knelt by the dead gunman and pried his Tanto from the corpse. "But I'd sure like to know why."

"Maybe one of these blokes can tell us," McCarter mused, glancing down at the motionless figures. "Then again, maybe they're all dead."

"This dude's still alive," James stated as he checked the opponent with the broken jaw. He pulled the unconscious man's wrists behind his back and prepared to cuff him. As the man's sleeve slipped up, James noticed a tattoo on the man's forearm. "Holy shit. I just found part of the answer."

"What is it?" Encizo asked, moving closer to see what James had found.

"The tattoo of a three-headed snake," James announced. "The symbol of TRIO. Our old sparring partners must know we're in town."

"TRIO?" McCarter said with disbelief. "We're not even looking for those bastards this time. What the hell are they coming after us for?"

"I thought we already solved that," Encizo remarked. "They want to kill us. What I'd like to know is how they identified us and located us so quickly."

"Yeah," James said grimly. "And I wonder how long it'll take before they try again."

7

Kaiju Hideo wished he had a cigarette. The yakuza *oyabun* had quit smoking two years before, but he still wanted a nicotine fix when he found himself in a high-stress situation. As he rode in the back seat of the white Mercedes-Benz with Matsuno Sadatoshi, Kaiju felt lots of stress. In fact, he felt as though he would have a nervous breakdown before the night was over.

They were ten miles from Tokyo. Kaiju was familiar with the area. His house was located a couple of miles to the west of the road the Mercedes traveled. Kaiju thought they might suddenly turn onto a side road and head for his home, but the car rolled to the east. The area was quiet, remarkably remote and lightly populated for Japan. That didn't comfort Kaiju, who knew that the best place for murder was a private, lonely spot without witnesses.

The Mercedes headed toward a pagodalike building surrounded by a tall stone wall. Kaiju recognized the building, which was a sixteenth-century temple that had belonged to an obscure Buddhist sect. The temple had survived bombing during the second world war, sustaining only slight damage. Plans had been drawn up to tear it down to make room for a housing-development project back in the middle of the 1960s, but attempts to protect the historic monument delayed the project. Finally in 1969 the temple and surrounding property were purchased by a wealthy eccentric.

Kaiju recalled that the temple had been occupied by quiet young men who claimed it was a religious retreat. Lights were in evidence at night, so outsiders knew the owners had installed electrical wiring, probably powered by diesel generators. No one knew much about it except that the temple personnel kept to themselves and didn't allow outsiders into their private world.

However, as the Mercedes approached the building, Kaiju realized that the temple was more than a private religious retreat. He now understood the reason for secrecy within the temple. Obviously the place had been purchased by the Snake Clan yakuza and now housed TRIO's temporary headquarters.

The gates of the temple wall were open, and the car rolled across the threshold. Kaiju noticed two sentries by the gate, both of them armed with Heckler & Koch assault rifles equipped with state-of-the-art night-vision scopes. An American-made Bell helicopter stood on a landing pad near the temple. Three gunmen waited for the Mercedes at the stone steps of the building. The car came to a halt, and Matsuno Sadatoshi opened a door and emerged from the vehicle, his *katana* in his fist.

Kaiju followed his example and left the car. The guards watched him with suspicion. He noticed they were armed with 9 mm Shin Chuo Kogyo submachine guns, Japanese weapons that resemble the old German Schmeisser MP-40 with a thicker barrel and improved hooded front sights and elevated L-type rear sights. The rear sights are adjustable, and the Shin Chuo Kogyo can fire with fair accuracy to about 200 yards.

"I'm afraid you'll have to be searched for weapons before you may enter, Kaiju-*san*," Matsuno explained.

"I understand," Kaiju assured him, well aware he had no choice in the matter, anyway.

The men were quite professional. They frisked him quickly, checking for weapons at the small of his back, ankles, between the shoulder blades and crotch. Of course, Kaiju had come to the meeting unarmed. To do otherwise would be foolish and would make TRIO suspicious. The guards finally nodded with approval and allowed Kaiju and Matsuno to enter the temple.

Two men waited for them in the hallway inside. One was a small, slightly built Japanese with a trim Hitler-style mustache above his lip. The other man was larger and very muscular. His hair was clipped very close to his round skull, and he held two steel balls in his hand, working the metal spheres around in circles with his constantly moving fingers. The balls clicked repeatedly as they tapped together in tiny orbits within the big man's palm.

Kaiju had seen steel balls used this way before—in kung fu movies. He realized such balls were used by some practitioners of certain forms of Chinese martial arts. The big man's hands revealed he was skilled in *chuan fa*. The knuckles had thick calluses, and his fingertips were tough and leathery.

"Kaiju-*san*," Matsuno began, "may I introduce two of our members from the United States. Andrew Tanaka and Harold Kuming. They were in charge of TRIO operations in San Francisco, California, until two and a half years ago when that branch of TRIO suffered a terrible defeat at the hands of the five men we are currently threatened by here in Japan."

"There were six of them, Matsuno-*san*," Tanaka, the smaller man, stated. "The five men you described, and a man dressed in black ninja costume. A man skilled in the arts of *ninjutsu*."

"A ninja in San Francisco?" Kaiju inquired, his eyes wide with surprise. Then he recalled that John Trent lived in San Franciso.

"Hai," Tanaka confirmed.

"Tanaka-*san* was the comrade I mentioned to you, Kaiju-*san*," Matsuno explained. "The one who stupidly left an American-made *tanto* knife in the body of Nagano's bodyguard."

"There is no need to be insulting," Tanaka said stiffly. His nose was still swollen and misshapen from the karate chop delivered by the bodyguard he had killed that night. "It was the sort of accident anyone might make."

"It may in fact prove to be a blessing in disguise, Tanaka-*san*," Matsuno replied. "Kuming-*san* is not impolite. He does not speak or understand Japanese. He is a Chinese American, formerly with the Black

Serpent Tong in San Francisco. When the tong became part of TRIO, Kuming-*san* entered our ranks.''

"I am pleased to meet you," Kaiju told Tanaka and Kuming, speaking English because he assumed both men would understand the language.

"Keep your mind working in English, Mr. Kaiju," Matsuno announced. "When we meet with the leaders of TRIO, everyone must converse in English. Strange as it may seem, the three men who run the greatest criminal network of Asia do not speak each other's language, yet all three speak English."

"I shall bear that in mind," Kaiju promised.

"You'd better," Matsuno warned.

All four men walked to a door at the end of the hall, where three guards were on duty. One was Japanese, another Chinese and the third was a Mongol. They nodded mute greetings to the group of four.

Matsuno reluctantly handed his sword to the Japanese guard.

"Please treat this *katana* with respect and care," he urged. "I value it more than life itself. Your life, as well as mine."

"It shall be safe, Matsuno-*san*," the sentry assured him.

They opened the doors and entered a large room. The scent of jasmine incense filled their nostrils as they approached three men seated on a platform. Kaiju was stunned by the appearance of the three leaders of TRIO.

Modern yakuza wear business suits and meet in air-conditioned office buildings. They discuss business in conference rooms, possibly using charts and video screens as visual aids. Yet the leaders of TRIO had chosen to meet with them in a dark room illuminated only by candles, with incense burning instead of ten-dollar cigars.

Kaiju was especially surprised by the costumes worn by TRIO's high commanders. A fat middle-aged Chinese was dressed in a green *mang p'ao* dragon robe with a purple jacket and a *ling t'ou* court collar that flared out from his shoulders like the roof of a pagoda.

The Chinese wore a Mandarin cap with a peacock-feather tassel and a *pu fang* coat of arms hung from his neck, bearing the three-headed black-serpent symbol of TRIO. His hands gripped the armrests of a thronelike chair, displaying fingernails at least four inches long. Wang Tse-Tu didn't bother to introduce himself. There was no need for Kaiju to know his name.

Tosha Khan didn't share his identity with Kaiju, either. The Mongol leader was a large muscular man with a fierce face and a drooping black mustache laced with silver hairs. He wore a bloodred robe with gold fringes and a brass helmet with hornlike ornaments above his brow. His wrists and forearms were covered by bronze chain mail. A three-headed snake amulet hung from his neck.

The third leader of TRIO was a well-built Japanese with iron-gray hair. His shoulders and arms were well-muscled from years of *kenjutsu* training. The *katana* of his ancestors rested along the armrest of his throne.

Kaiju had never met Shimo Goro before, but he was certain this man was the leader of the powerful Snake Clan yakuza.

Shimo's costume wasn't as elaborate as that of the other two TRIO leaders. The *oyabun* of the Snake Clan wore a black kimono jacket and matching *hakama* culottes. A green and blue fan was thrust into a gold obi sash around his waist. Shimo also wore an amulet with the symbol of TRIO.

Under different circumstances, these three men would have seemed ridiculous. Yet their costumes seemed perfectly suited for them. They were three Oriental emperors, supreme commanders of the most powerful Asian crime network in the world. They were all powerful in that room, godlike in their ability to declare life or death for anyone standing before them. The setting was bizarre and frightening. Kaiju felt as if he had stepped back in time and arrived in an age when a man could lose his head if he failed to bow deeply enough to please a member of royalty.

"Greetings, Mr. Kaiju," Shimo Goro declared. "And welcome to TRIO. I'm certain your yakuza clan shall prosper from this association."

"I am looking forward to this, Shimo-*san*," Kaiju replied with a deep bow, hand extended like a beggar's, yakuza-style.

"You will address him as Shimo-*sama*," Matsuno whispered harshly.

Kaiju bristled at the demand. He was accustomed to giving orders and being treated with considerable respect, but he never insisted his *kobun* give him the title *lord*, and he did not care to address Shimo as if the TRIO leader was a *daimyo*, "warlord." But an error in acceptable behavior could be fatal under the circumstances.

"I pledge my everlasting loyalty, Shimo-*sama*," Kaiju declared quickly. "My yakuza clan shall do whatever you wish."

"They haven't done very well so far," Tosha Khan said grimly. "Your men tried to kill three individuals who are among TRIO's worst enemies. Your people failed. We received word that they attempted this assassination with knives and a sword. Only one man carried a gun. Who did they think they were trying to kill? Three prostitutes who were holding out on payment to their pimp?"

"I beg your pardon, My Lord," Kaiju began. "But the two men in charge of that assassination attempt were sent to the Kin-Rakooda plant by order from Matsuno-*san*. They were in charge of the attempt. My *kobun* simply assisted and followed orders."

"That is accurate," Matsuno admitted.

"You rushed the task, Matsuno-*san*," Shimo remarked thoughtfully. "You ordered your men to kill the enemy as soon as they saw them. That was careless. We cannot afford to be careless with such dangerous men. Your men made mistakes, and they paid for it with their lives. The assassination of our five adversaries must be carefully planned and executed to insure success."

"I think we should wait," Wang Tse-Tu stated. "We do not know why these five men are in Tokyo."

"They have come to destroy our plans," Tosha Khan snapped. "They've done so in the past. Somehow they always learn when we're planning a major operation, and they find a way to ruin everything. They stopped our plan to seize control of drug traffic in San Francisco. They wrecked our scheme to finance TRIO operations with gold in the Philippines. Most recently they ruined our effort to use a Soviet biological weapon to blackmail and coerce nations...."

"That was a scheme that never should have happened," Shimo said in a hard voice. "And you are discussing matters that these men have no need to know."

"They should know that my son Temujin was killed by these bastards," Tosha Khan declared angrily. "I will personally reward whoever kills them. I will pay their assassins one million dollars in any currency they choose."

"I will kill them for free," Matsuno declared. "They escaped my *katana* once. It will not happen again. I lost face because of them, and honor dictates that I must have revenge for the failure they caused me. If I fail again, I swear to commit *seppuku* rather than live with dishonor again."

"Cutting your belly open isn't going to solve anything," Wang Tse-Tu stated. "And killing those five isn't going to help, either, if it brings Kompei down on our heads. You did say a Kompei agent was with the pair that came to your office, Kaiju-*san*?"

"That is correct," Kaiju confirmed.

"Perhaps we should suspend activities for now," Wang suggested. "Until we are certain of better odds for success. With those mysterious warriors in Tokyo, we are facing a threat we had not expected."

"Allow the murderers of my son to go free?" Tosha Khan banged his fist against the arm of his chair. The chain mail at his wrist scored a deep mark in the wood. "Absolutely not! We have an opportunity to destroy them, and I insist that we remain here in Japan until they are dead."

"You would jeopardize our entire organization for revenge." Wang shook his head. "My people have a saying about revenge. Before you set out to seek it, you should first dig *two* graves. In this case, dig five and an enormous pit for TRIO."

"What do you say, Goro?" Tosha demanded.

"I say one of you wishes to act too rashly and the other thinks we should do nothing," Shimo answered with a sigh. "Either path will lead to our downfall. If we strike too quickly, try too hard to find these five mystery men, we will surely make mistakes and waste needless energy on them. Do not forget, our original purpose for coming to Japan is to unite all the yakuza clans and make them part of TRIO."

"Many will never agree to that, Shimo-*sama*," Kaiju warned.

"We know that," Shimo answered. "That's why Nagano had to die. We ordered him to contact the Green Tiger Clan with our demands that they join us. He did so and came back with a refusal. So we told him he had to betray the Tigers if he wished to survive. He did not join us, so we killed him—more as an example to the Green Tiger Clan than because he refused us. After all, the man wasn't that important . . . or so we thought at the time. But he may have been important enough to come to the attention of whoever those five commandos work for."

"I have a theory about that, Shimo-*sama*," Matsuno remarked.

"Perhaps later," Shimo replied. "The fact is, we cannot afford to take no action at all. We've already started an offense against the Green Tiger Clan. If we fail to follow through with that action, they will move against us. This must be our primary concern. If the five warriors present a problem, we deal with them then."

"There may be six opponents to deal with," Kaiju remarked. "Tanaka-*san* mentioned a ninja from San Francisco. Such a man is here in Japan. He's an enemy of my clan, and his uncle in San Francisco is a traitor who refuses to obey orders to extend our yakuza operations to include narcotics and prostitution."

"Sounds to me like he's simply someone you want to get rid of," Wang commented.

"His name is John Trent, and he killed seven of my men this morning," Kaiju declared. "He's a ninja, trained here in Japan by Kaiju ninja...members of my own clan. Those two Occidentals claiming to be Interpol agents know Trent. They were looking for him."

"That's true," Matsuno confirmed. "I saw and heard everything that went on in his office. In fact, that's how I guessed the bastards might show up at the Kin-Rakooda plant."

"Then perhaps you can guess where they might go next," Tosha Khan suggested with a cold smile.

8

Japan is actually a network of islands. The largest is Honshu, which contains most of the major cities, including Tokyo, Kyoto, Osaka and Yokohama. The northernmost island is Hokkaido, and Shikoku and Kyushu are located to the south. Besides the four large islands of Japan proper, the Ryukyu Islands and more than a thousand smaller islands are also part of Japan.

The forest was located in Shikoku. Conifer trees and bamboo grew in abundance, and a lake and several streams provided plenty of fresh water. The area was quiet, remote and very private. It was also the base for a handful of Kaiju ninja still living in Japan.

John Trent knelt on a tatami mat, facing Kaiju Shintaro. The old man sat as still as a statue. Trent had no idea what the sensei's age might be. The ancient ninja chief appeared not to have changed since Trent last saw him ten years before. Shintaro was a small man, his skin wrinkled with age, and the long whiskers flowing from his chin were as white as new-fallen snow. But Shintaro's eyes were youthful and alert. There was certainly nothing wrong with the old man's mind.

Shintaro sat on a cushion in the main training hall. He nodded his bald-shaved head occasionally as he listened to Trent explain the situation concerning Kaiju Hideo and the yakuza. Shintaro considered the matter in silence. Trent didn't speak, patiently waiting for the old man to make a decision.

"Hideo is my nephew," Kaiju Shintaro said at last. "My brother's eldest son. After the war, my brother and I parted company because we had differing views about the future of the Kaiju Clan. As you know, I continued our family tradition of *ninjutsu* while my brother started a yakuza clan. I felt he was wrong to do this, but at least my brother retained a sense of honor, and his *kobun* were required to uphold those principles."

Shintaro shook his head sadly. "Last month, my brother died," he continued. "His sons took over the yakuza branch of the Kaiju Clan. Hideo and his younger brother Matso have no sense of honor, no principles. They are a disgrace to the Kaiju family. The demands that they have made of the yakuza clan and your uncle Inoshiro are inexcusable."

"You know what I must do," Trent said softly. It wasn't a question. Shintaro knew the issues at stake.

"Hideo and Matso must be stopped," the old man declared. "They are family. I cannot get directly involved. You understand this, John?"

"*Hai,*" Trent assured him. "I would not ask you to get involved. I have come to explain what I must do and to ask your forgiveness."

"My forgiveness?" Shintaro raised his white eyebrows.

"Hideo is going to have me killed," Trent explained. "He will also order his *kobun* to murder my uncle in the United States. I have to kill Hideo. My life and Inoshiro's life will be taken otherwise. I have no choice."

"And you want me to forgive you for killing my nephew before you have done so?" The old man seemed amused. "What if I refused to forgive you?"

"Then I would not leave here alive."

"You came here although you knew I might have you killed?" Shintaro asked. "A dangerous risk, John."

"If I killed Hideo, you would have realized I did it," Trent answered. "And if you wanted me dead, you'd find me eventually. You or your ninja agents would hunt me down and kill me. If I am to die by your hand, sensei, I would rather die now before causing you any grief."

"So what you really want is my permission," the old man mused. "You will also have to kill Matso. Both brothers must die for you and Inoshiro to be safe."

"Very well," Trent said with a nod.

"Try to kill them quickly," Shintaro said with a sigh. "After all, they are family."

"I understand," Trent assured him. "You taught me well, sensei. A ninja must sometimes kill, but he should do it quickly without sadistic joy. Their deaths shall be swift."

"Thank you, John," the old man replied. "What weapons do you have?"

"I have two pistols taken from Hideo's *kobun*," Trent answered. "I can improvise other tools and weapons."

"No need for that." Shintaro rose to his feet, holding a thick oak stave for support. "Come with me, John."

Trent followed Shintaro to a platform at the opposite side of the room. More than a dozen swords were mounted on the wall, none of them traditional samurai swords. The weapons were encased in plain black scabbards. The handles were wrapped in sharkskin and twisted black silk, and the hand guards were plain, unlike the finely decorated and ornate guards of a classic *katana* or *wakazashi* short sword. The *ninja-do*, the sword of the ninja, wasn't a cherished work of art, but a practical weapon and tool. The hand guard was black, large enough to provide additional protection for the user's hands, and square-shaped to block or trap an opponent's weapon. The blade was slightly shorter than a *katana* long sword's, and unlike samurai weapons, straight with a slanted point.

Trent was very familiar with such swords, having used the *ninja-do* many times in the past. Shintaro selected a sword from the wall and handed it to the American ninja. Trent held the weapon in both hands and bowed his forehead to the scabbard.

"Domo arigato, sensei," Trent said with profound thanks.

"Open the drawers beneath this platform," Shintaro instructed. "You will find other equipment that may prove useful."

Trent obeyed. The first drawer contained an assortment of steel throwing stars, spikes, knives, caltrops and needles. The next contained clawlike devices for hands and feet, fighting chains with weighted ends, sickle weapons with sharp curved blades, chains extending from the butts of metal handles and *tonfa* fighting sticks.

The third drawer held other weapons of *ninjutsu*. Packets of small steel balls, darts and bamboo blow guns, *nunchaku* flails, *sai* weapons with trident blades and *kama* fighting hatchets. Trent was familiar with all these devices. He was more skilled with some than others, but he was competent with them all to some degree at least. With others, including the *ninja-do*, Trent was indeed a master.

"Take what you feel you may need," Shintaro told him. "We also have archery equipment, firearms and ninja clothing, if you wish to use them. You may want to make some *metsubushi* or take some poisons from the laboratory. None of these items can be traced back to us, so take whatever you wish and discard these tools when you have completed your mission."

"You are too generous, sensei," Trent replied. His eyes were moist. He was truly moved by the assistance of his old master. The fact that Shintaro knew that Trent would use these weapons to kill his nephews made the gesture all the more meaningful. "I cannot hope to ever thank you properly for what you are doing for me.''

"Your uncle is a very close friend," Shintaro stated. "At one time he was a fine ninja warrior, yet even he strayed from the path. He never disgraced and dishonored us as my nephews have done, but Inoshiro strayed nonetheless. However, you are truly ninja, John. You have always lived by the principles and code of honor that separates the true ninja from a free-lance espionage agent or a hired assassin. Few understand this, but you hold this understanding in your mind and, most important, in your heart."

The old man placed a hand on Trent's shoulder. "One day soon," he continued, "I shall be unable to carry on the traditions of the Kaiju Ninja Clan. My students will continue to keep our traditions alive here in Japan, and you will carry on for us in the United States. Our countries are close allies, my son. You share a heritage that is both American and Japanese. Most important of all, you are our greatest hope to preserve the true way of *ninjutsu* in a modern world. When I help you, I am really helping the hope of the very future of my clan."

"I will do my best to uphold this duty," Trent promised.

"Your first duty is to your present mission," Shintaro reminded him. "I pray you will succeed. If not, I am confident you will die as you have lived. As a ninja with honor."

9

On August 6, 1945, the city of Hiroshima had found a tragic and permanent place in history. On that date, an atomic bomb was dropped on Hiroshima. It was the first time a nuclear weapon was employed in a military strike, and the incredible destructive force of the atomic explosion stunned the world. About a hundred-and-thirty thousand people were killed or seriously injured. More than four square miles of Hiroshima were destroyed—obliterated, as if assaulted by an army of flamethrowers.

When most people think of Hiroshima, they still recall the terrible photographs of victims of the atom bomb, people covered with hideous radiation burns. Crushed buildings and disfigured children are the images of Hiroshima that come to mind. Overlooking all these grisly mental pictures is the ominous mushroom cloud that has become the symbol of the ultimate technological terror of the twentieth century.

Yet Hiroshima is not simply a city of the past. It wasn't vaporized by the bomb. Hiroshima has been rebuilt and is a center for manufacturing and production; textiles, food processing and shipbuilding are among the major industries of Hiroshima. The population has more than doubled since 1945. Although generally regarded as a place of unspeakable destruction, Hiroshima is actually a remarkable survivor, a city that was consumed by radioactive brimstone and returned from hell, stronger than it was before.

The five men of Phoenix Force and Ikeda Ken arrived in Hiroshima shortly after midnight. The Kompei agent had supplied a helicopter, and McCarter piloted the chopper across the big island of Honshu, from Tokyo to the southwest coast to Hiroshima.

Ikeda had managed to satisfy the Tokyo police that the incident at the Kin-Rakooda Auto Corporation had been part of a joint investigation by Kompei and Interpol. Since James, McCarter and Encizo had all the necessary ID to convince the police that they were genuine Interpol agents, and Ikeda was the head of internal investigations for Kompei, the police reluctantly agreed not to hold the three Phoenix commandos for questioning.

They landed on a helicopter pad at Hiroshima Bay. The local police had been notified, and they had prepared for the arrival of Ikeda and his five mysterious Occidental friends. A car was waiting for them, a large black sedan with a uniformed policeman for a driver.

"Are you sure it's wise to meet with Sekizawa Sato with a car like this?" Katzenelenbogen asked the Kompei officer as they approached the sedan. "One look at the driver, and he'll know it's an unmarked police car."

"Sekizawa is not frightened by the police," Ikeda replied. "He's the top *oyabun* of one of the largest

yakuza clans in Japan. This is no secret, and Sekizawa is aware the police know about him. However,
his Green Tiger Clan gets most of its profits through
perfectly legal methods. Sekizawa is the president of
Tiger Mountain Sake, a very popular brand of sake.
Sold throughout the world."

"It seems all the yakuza *oyabun* run big corporations here in Japan," Gary Manning remarked, shaking his head with dismay. "And nobody seems very
surprised about it."

"True," Ikeda admitted. "The yakuza are behind
many of the largest corporations in Japan. But how
many American corporations and powerful organizations are actually run by criminal syndicates?"

"A lot more than most Americans realize," Calvin
James commented as he took a canvas rifle case to the
sedan. "Sometimes it's hard to tell the difference between so-called organized crime and good old-
fashioned American corruption."

"Corruption, criminal activity, terrorism and evil
schemes are part of the human race all over the
world," McCarter added, holding a briefcase as he
strolled to the car. "That's why we get to travel so
much."

"I wish you wouldn't have so much firepower,"
Ikeda Ken confessed, glancing at the valises carried by
McCarter, Katz and Encizo. He was aware that the
cases contained weapons. "After all, gentlemen, Sekizawa has agreed to meet us. He certainly doesn't intend to ambush us in a public place. That would be
very crude and stupid. Not his style at all."

"We're feeling a little insecure since TRIO tried to kill us," Rafael Encizo remarked dryly. "Try to humor us for now. When we feel a little safer, we won't be as heavily armed."

"I'm just concerned how Sekizawa will react when he finds out you're carrying an arsenal with automatic weapons," Ikeda declared as he climbed into the seat next to the driver. "He may become very nervous and cancel the meeting immediately."

"Calculated risk," Katz told the Kompei agent. "Let us worry about that."

"I would not be at all concerned if I was not present with you at this time," Ikeda admitted.

"Is there problem here?" the driver asked in broken English. He was young and obviously nervous. Like most Japanese police, he did not carry a gun and was armed only with a nightstick, but he understood enough of the conversation to realize the other men were packing firearms.

"Let us hope not," Ikeda replied in Japanese.

HIROSHIMA LOOKS LIKE any other industry-oriented city in Japan. It has a great abundance of factories and processing plants, but offers little for those seeking entertainment or nightlife. The main cultural product and virtually the only tourist attraction is the Peace Memorial Park.

The Japanese government officially declared Hiroshima a "shrine for peace" in 1949, but the Japanese people are far too practical to turn an entire city into a shrine—especially a city located along an open bay and surrounded by fertile valleys with crops of rice, wheat and bamboo. The Peace Memorial Park is the only concession to the city's status as a shrine. This consists of a monument to the dead, a marble tomb and the gutted remains of a nondescript building with a skeletal dome of twisted metal girders.

The park is the site of a huge demonstration for peace every August sixth, when thousands come from all over the world to participate in rallies and religious services that embrace many faiths, as well as nondenominational rituals. But as the sedan bearing Phoenix Force approached the Peace Memorial Park, the area was occupied only by a handful of people.

Two of the visitors were elderly Japanese, a man and a woman. They knelt by the cenotaph, palms pressed together in prayer as they burned incense to honor the dead. Another gray-haired Asian, dressed in an expensive European pin-striped suit, sat on a marble bench and stared solemnly at the ruins. He was surrounded by four young Japanese men, also in business suits, who seemed more concerned with watching the surrounding area than paying homage to the victims of the atom bomb.

It wasn't difficult to determine who Sekizawa Sato was among the group. The guy staring at the ruins was either the yakuza *oyabun* accompanied by four *kobun* bodyguards or a very paranoid government official who just happened to choose to visit the park at 12:30 a.m.

Phoenix Force and Ikeda Ken left the sedan and approached the semicircle of *kobun* guarding the yakuza boss. To ease Ikeda's fears and to lessen the odds of offending Sekizawa, James had left his rifle case in the car. Katz had also agreed to leave his briefcase with the driver, but McCarter and Encizo still carried their valises. The *kobun* glared suspiciously at the five men. Two of the hoods unbuttoned their jackets, no doubt to have their guns close at hand if they felt threatened by the strangers.

Ikeda greeted Sekizawa in formal Japanese, then continued, "We are grateful that you agreed to meet with us, and we apologize for any inconvenience this may have caused."

"Is not problem for me," the gray-haired man announced as he turned his head to look over his shoulder at the group. "I come here often. My parents died here when they dropped the bomb. Father was a fisherman. A shark had maimed his arm when he was young, so he did not serve in the military. He never cared much for soldiers, anyway."

Sekizawa rose. He was tall for a Japanese, nearly six foot. His neatly trimmed mustache, horn-rimmed glasses and three-piece suit suggested he might be a banker or a lawyer. Sekizawa certainly didn't look like a gangster. He smiled at Phoenix Force.

"My father thought the war was a mistake," he continued. "He considered Tojo a dangerous fanatic, Mussolini a conceited pig and Hitler an outright lunatic. Father wept when Pearl Harbor was attacked. He said the Americans would retaliate with a mighty vengeance. He was certainly right about that."

"War is always a nasty business," Katz remarked.

"I know," Sekizawa said with a nod. "I was in the Imperial Navy in the Philippines. That was all very nasty, indeed. Still, if my father had been in charge of Japan, Hiroshima might never have been bombed. This city had unfortunate karma at the time, but for the last forty-two years, Hiroshima has not done badly."

Calvin James gazed at the ruined building near the monuments. It was pitted and crumbled, in danger of collapsing if one breathed too hard on the ancient framework. The charred marks on the walls still bore the reminder of the nuclear fury that had devastated the city. James wondered what it had been like for the people of Hiroshima when the world exploded into sheets of fire and the air became deadly poison. It must have seemed as though Hell itself had erupted from the bomb and the Devil had come to punish the innocent as savagely as the guilty.

"Ah," Sekizawa began, turning toward James. "You are intrigued by the ruins? Actually, the bomb wrecked that building, but time and harsh weather have contributed to the wretched condition of that sorrowful structure. You see, the city administration has not bothered to try to maintain the place. Opinions vary about this shrine. Some feel all the old buildings should be torn down and replaced. They say 'Why preserve the memories of such horror?' Others believe we should have kept many ruined structures as a memorial to that terrible day and a reminder to the entire world that nuclear weapons must never be used again. So the administration decided to compromise.

They kept that wreck, but have not tried to preserve it.
Eventually, it will fall apart on its own and only the
monuments of marble will remain. I rather wish it
would fall in. Perhaps I can purchase the land.''

"That's all very interesting, Mr. Sekizawa," Katz
stated. "But we have little time, and the business we
wish to discuss is important. Please understand, our
haste is not due to lack of respect or rudeness."

"I fear I have been rude, gentlemen," Sekizawa said
with a polite bow. "However, Hiroshima is a passion
for me. I helped establish some of the first businesses
here, and I still live in the area. Tokyo and Osaka are
the bases of many businesses in Japan—too many.
Hiroshima will one day be known as the second capi-
tal of Japan. But, to business. How may I help you?"

"Maybe we can help each other," Gary Manning
replied. "An associate of the Green Tiger Clan was
murdered a while back. Nagano Jiro, the vice
president of the Kin-Rakooda Corporation."

"I know of the incident," Sekizawa said, nodding.
"But my clan had nothing to do with his death."

"We think we know who had Nagano murdered,"
Katz told him. "Are you familiar with an organization called TRIO? The Snake Clan is part of it. Possibly the Kaiju yakuza has also become connected with
the TRIO network."

The *oyabun* shook his head. "These are matters best
said in whispers. And I don't think I should discuss
these matters with you even with a tiny voice."

"Tiny voices can be hard to hear," James announced bluntly. "And I think you'd better listen to

us. TRIO tried to kill two of my partners and me this afternoon. They were assisted by *kobun* assassins from the Kaiju Clan, and we have reason to believe Kaiju Hideo himself tried to finger us for the hit. Am I using too much slang or can you follow me so far?''

''I understand,'' Sekizawa assured him. ''But I do not see why this concerns me.''

''The only motive anyone might have to kill Nagano was that he belonged to the Green Tiger Clan,'' Rafael Encizo explained. ''We suspect TRIO was responsible. Some evidence suggests Kaiju had a ninja from the United States assist on the hit. If Kaiju is with TRIO that means the latter outfit ordered the assassination. So, unless you want TRIO to control your clan in the future, I think you might have a pretty big problem on your hands. Nagano's death might be a warning for you to join TRIO.''

''Why would you assume that?'' Sekizawa inquired.

''Because the Kaiju Clan didn't have any connection with TRIO until recently,'' James answered. ''Apparently this changed shortly after the previous Kaiju leader croaked and Hideo took over. TRIO wouldn't be interested in recruiting a little outfit like the Kaiju Clan unless it was a stepping-stone to bigger things. Maybe gaining control of the Green Tiger Clan.''

''So you've come to warn me of possible danger?'' the *oyabun* said with a smile. ''Yet you gentlemen are policemen. International policemen, perhaps, but hardly the sort who would wish to help me.''

"The Green Tiger Clan has a reputation for dealing in gambling, prostitution, minor black market and fencing stolen merchandise," Ikeda declared. "You bribe officials, pay off judges and do other illegal things. But your clan was never involved in narcotics and avoided crimes of violence or actual robbery. TRIO, however, resorts to violence and murder frequently. They deal in heroin and other narcotics and even attempted to use a stolen germ-warfare formula for criminal purposes. Obviously, we would rather have your Green Tiger Clan operating here in Japan than TRIO."

"For now," Sekizawa said with a shrug. "I believe our conversation is over, gentlemen. Good luck and—"

Calvin James suddenly dove at Sekizawa Sato and dragged him to the ground. Bullets hissed above their prone bodies and ricocheted sourly from the marble tomb beyond. The chattering roar of two automatic weapons ripped the stillness of the night. The muzzle flash of the chatterguns flickered orange light across the tormented face of one of the *kobun*. Two bullets meant for the *oyabun* had struck the bodyguard in the chest.

The other four members of Phoenix Force had also seen the gunmen approach from a green van across the street from the park. Katz grabbed Ikeda's arm and yanked him down. Gary Manning immediately dropped flat on his stomach and drew a .357 Magnum Eagle autoloading pistol from his jacket. The Canadian marksman was a better shot with a rifle, but he had to work with what he had. Manning gripped the Eagle in both hands, aimed carefully and fired.

A 158-grain wadcutter slug tore into the belly of the gunman Manning had targeted for termination. The Magnum-powered .357 round bore through the assassin like an ice pick through soft mush. The bullet struck backbone and shattered the fifth lumbar vertebra. The killer dropped the Shin Chuo Kogyo submachine gun and collapsed, his body twitching helplessly before submitting to oblivion.

David McCarter dove to the ground, drawing his Browning Hi-Power automatic while still in midair. A salvo of enemy bullets narrowly missed the Briton's hurtling form. A slug tugged at his pant leg and creased his left calf. The British ace barely felt the sting of hot metal against flesh as he hit the ground, snap-aimed his Browning and triggered it twice.

The pistol marksman from London pumped both 9 mm parabellum rounds into the upper body of the second gunman. One projectile punctured a lung, while the other messenger of death punched through the man's throat and blasted a gory exit hole at the nape. The killer sprawled backward, arms and legs splayed wide apart as if signaling that his life was finished and he had no objections.

Another Green Tiger *kobun* fell. The long shaft of an arrow jutted from the dead man's chest. Calvin James pulled his Colt Commander from shoulder leather as he clutched Sekizawa's elbow in his other hand and helped the older man run for cover. James and the *oyabun* headed for the shelter behind the big marble tomb.

They dashed around the corner of the great stone casket. A flash of silver lightning streaked toward James's gun hand. The sword struck the frame of his .45 pistol and chopped the Colt Commander out of the black warrior's fist. Luckily it didn't hack off a finger in the process.

"Shit!" James cried. The oath became a shout as he swung a sword-foot kick to the ambusher's right forearm.

The tae kwon-do technique sent the would-be assassin spinning off balance. The blade of his crude homemade sword clanged against marble. The killer was clad in black with a ninja-style scarf mask, but James had no doubt that he was really a yakuza in disguise. The black hardass had tangled with ninja before and knew that he wasn't dealing with one of the shadow warriors. The man was a sword-swinging thug.

James swiftly grabbed his opponent's wrists to push the sword away from himself and rammed a knee kick into the killer's abdomen. The yakuza hit man gasped breathlessly, and James pulled his arms upward as he turned to place his buttocks against the thug's hip. The sword wavered overhead, the blade cutting air as the killer held on to the handle.

The Phoenix pro bent forward and drew his arms downward in a roundhouse swing to avoid lancing himself with the sword. The yakuza attacker hurled over James's buttocks and back to land hard on his knees. James twisted his opponent's wrists, finally forcing him to release the sword.

The long blade clattered at the marble base of the tomb. James slashed a karate *shuto* stroke to the hoodlum's face. The side of his hand smashed into the assassin's upper lip. The enemy yakuza fell on his back, blood flowing from his mouth. James quickly stomped on the man's solar plexus, driving his boot heel upward into the chest cavity. The power of the ruthless kick ruptured the heart, and the killer suffered a massive cardiac arrest and expired two seconds later.

There was the roar of a gun close to James, and his body reacted by an involuntary jerking of his spine, contorting his body in a massive nervous shrug. A voice cried out, and James saw another black-clad figure fall to the ground. Suddenly Yakov Katzenelenbogen appeared next to James. The Israeli held a 9 mm SIG-Sauer P-226 pistol in his left fist. A wisp of smoke curled up from the muzzle.

"Thanks, man." James sighed with relief.

"My pleasure," Katz assured him.

An automatic weapon bellowed from the shadows surrounding the ruins of the A-bomb blasted building. The unseen gunman was a bad shot and opened up with too much haste. His spray of 9 mm slugs struck too high, whining against the stone surface of the tomb.

Katz and Ikeda Ken returned fire, aiming at the muzzle flash of their opponent's weapon. The Israeli's P-226 and the Kompei agent's Nambu Model 57 belched four 9 mm parabellum projectiles into the general area of the sniper's position. At least one bullet hit the mark. An ugly sound that resembled a mingling of an animal yelping in pain and a man's cry of helpless rage erupted from the shadows. The sniper didn't fire his weapon again.

"Bastards got us surrounded," James muttered as he scooped up his fallen .45 Colt.

"I noticed that, too," Katz replied, his voice remarkably calm. The others often wondered if Katz could really switch off his fear in combat because he always seemed cool-headed in the face of danger. Had they asked the Israeli, he would have told them "absolutely not," unashamed to admit it.

Two shapes suddenly appeared at the opposite end of the tomb. James, Katz and Ikeda pointed their weapons at the figures but held their fire when the other men raised their hands.

"Matteh kudasai!" they cried in unison.

"They're my *kobun*!" Sekizawa told the others. "Hold your fire!"

The Phoenix Force trio and Ikeda lowered their pistols. The two Green Tiger yakuza sighed with relief and approached the group.

"Matteh kudasai!" a voice rasped behind the Tiger bodyguards.

The two assumed that one of their comrades had followed their example and had joined the others behind the tomb. The Green Tiger hoods turned toward the voice.

A machine gun snarled. Parabellum slugs tore through the flesh of the two yakuza defenders. Sekizawa watched with mute horror as his men convulsed wildly and fell lifeless, their bodies ravaged and bloodied.

"Sneaky bastard," James hissed as he aimed his Colt Commander and squeezed off two shots at the machine gunner in the shadows.

Katz and Ikeda also opened fire. The gunman whirled about from the impact of multiple bullet wounds. His spinning body absorbed two more 9 mm parabellums and an extra .45 slug. The man was thoroughly dead before he collapsed.

"Party's still going on here, too?" McCarter commented as he scrambled behind the tomb. The Briton still carried his briefcase in one fist and his Browning Hi-Power in the other. "We've still got company at the front door, too."

"How is our side holding up?" Katz inquired.

"I didn't see any of our team get hit," McCarter replied as he opened his briefcase and removed a compact M-10 Ingram machine pistol. "But I think all of Sekizawa's men are dead."

"What about the cop in the sedan?" James asked.

"Didn't see anyone attack the car," the Briton answered, making certain his Ingram was fully loaded and ready for action. "But to be honest, I forgot all about the bloke. I was sort of busy."

"Maybe the enemy didn't think about him, either," James mused. "I sure hope that kid has enough sense to call for reinforcements and he doesn't try anything stupid.''

"Who are these men trying to kill?" Sekizawa inquired as he knelt next to the marble shelter. "Your group or me?"

"Right now that isn't important," Katz replied, peering around the edge of the tomb. "They obviously intend to kill all of us anyway, so who the main target might be is a moot point for now."

"Yeah," James added. "The only thing we have to worry about right now is staying alive."

More attackers had emerged from the green van across the street, and others were already scattered around the area. Their strategy seemed to be simple enough. Surround Phoenix Force, Ikeda and Sekizawa and catch them in a cross fire or corral them to be ambushed by killers positioned behind the tomb or stationed at the A-bomb ruins.

Manning and Encizo were closer to the cenotaph than the tomb. The Canadian and Cuban headed for the monument and ducked behind it.

Without warning, the enemy opened fire from all directions, their rifles and handguns spitting blistering volleys. The attackers in front of the monuments used the van for cover, and others sheltered behind tree trunks. The snipers in the ruins were once again delivering a deadly barrage of automatic fire.

Phoenix Force, along with Ikeda, ignored the fire spewing from the direction of the van. Relying on the marble structures to shield them from bullets from that direction, Katz and Ikeda concentrated on the opponents to the right while Encizo and Manning kept the enemy at the left busy. McCarter shoved a spare magazine to the Ingram machine pistol into his belt and turned to Calvin James.

"What d'ya say we cover each other?" the Briton asked.

"The others seem sorta busy," James agreed. "Leapfrog?"

"I'll be first frog," McCarter told him. "Hope we don't croak. Eh, mate?"

"R-r-ibbit," the black man replied, imitating a frog. "Let's go show these dudes who's king of the lily pad."

The joking was a way of releasing tension. Neither man was actually amused by the possibility of being shot to pieces before they could get three yards from the tomb. They didn't take the job lightly and weren't overconfident about the chances of success, but staying put was almost as dangerous as running into the open. The risk-taking was for the sake of their teammates as well as themselves. None of the men of Phoenix Force would ever hesitate to risk his life to save the others.

"Wait, damn it!" Katz shouted as McCarter dashed toward the building.

"Things ain't gonna get better unless we change it," James replied. The black commando hurried after McCarter, his Colt Commander in one fist and Nambu pistol in the other.

"He's right, you know," Ikeda shouted as he ducked low in response to a chip of marble that flew past his face.

"Should have waited for a lull in the shooting," Katz muttered, speaking more to himself than Ikeda because he realized the Kompei agent was right.

"We might all be dead before that happens," Ikeda remarked. He had heard Katz, anyway.

Suddenly another burst of automatic fire exploded from the street. But the bullets weren't aimed at Phoenix Force. A hail of high-velocity projectiles tore into a trio of gunmen who lurked behind some trees to the left of the cenotaph. One enemy triggerman fell, both hands clutching his bullet-torn side. Three slugs had punched through his rib cage to tear into the chest cavity and gouge a trio of messy exit wounds from the center of his chest.

Another enemy gunsel staggered away from the cover of a tree trunk. Blood spurted from a severed artery at his collarbone. His arm hung limply as his submachine gun dragged uselessly along the grass. Gary Manning spotted the guy, aimed his Magnum pistol, but hesitated because the man didn't present an immediate threat.

Rafael Encizo didn't share the Canadian's sense of fair play. Encizo knew the enemy intended to butcher them in cold blood. They had picked the fight, and Encizo figured they deserved whatever they got. He fired two 9 mm rounds into the wounded man's upper torso. One parabellum shattered the gunman's sternum and the other drilled through his heart.

Manning turned toward the source of the unexpected friendly fire. The young police officer who had driven them to the park had emerged from the sedan and removed Calvin James's M-16 assault rifle from its canvas case. Crouching by the car, he adopted a kneeling stance and fired at the enemy forces in the trees.

The third gunman answered the policeman with a Heckler & Koch assault rifle. Bullets raked the sedan, puncturing the steel frame and shattering glass. The officer sprawled on his belly, visibly shaken by the close brush with death. He wasn't a coward: he was merely inexperienced with combat and untrained to handle such a situation. Given that background, the young officer had displayed enormous courage.

The enemy with the H&K became very bold and stepped away from cover as he fired at the policeman. Manning peered through the sights of his Eagle pistol until the blade of the frontsight found the side of the gunman's head. Manning had no problem with taking a killer out to save someone's life. He squeezed the trigger and blasted a 158 grain slug into the thug's skull. Bone burst apart, spraying brain matter before the corpse hit the ground.

Although the threat from the assailants positioned behind the trees had been terminated, the others continued the battle with increased fury. The gunmen at the enemy van hosed the sedan with a murderous swarm of high-velocity slugs. Holes appeared in the windshield, and the glass spiderwebbed before it fell apart.

Other bullets punctured the radiator and shattered the headlights. Projectiles scraped the car hood and pierced the upholstery inside the vehicle. The policeman stayed down, pinned by the assault, but fairly well sheltered by the steel body of the big automobile.

Two of the gunmen stationed at the trees to the right of the tomb were armed with Shin Chuo Kogyo submachine guns, and the third carried a .45 caliber 1911A1 Colt pistol. One machine gunner strafed Phoenix Force's position while the other aimed his weapon at the policeman by the sedan. A stream of 9 mm rounds raked the cop's position. Four bullets tore a vicious row of ragged holes in the young officer's chest, the impact shoving his body against the right front tire. The enemy nailed him with another volley that chopped his upper torso into a bloodied glob of butchered flesh and shattered bone.

Yakov Katzenelenbogen remained in a prone position as bullets sliced air above his head. The Israeli aimed his SIG-Sauer at the bastard who'd burned the young cop. Bracing the pistol along his prosthesis, Katz aimed carefully and fired two rounds.

Both parabellum rounds tore into the gunman's forearm. The violent force of the high-velocity slugs ripped flesh and muscle and smashed bone. The Shin Chuo Kogyo flew from the hood's hands as he screamed and stumbled away from the cover of a tree. Ikeda spotted the wounded man and pumped two Nambu rounds into his chest. The dying thug fell, but his companions continued to fire at the defenders' position.

CALVIN JAMES and David McCarter had been occupied by making a dash to the bombed-out building. McCarter ran forward first, dispatching a brief volley at the gunmen hidden among the ruins. Then he immediately performed a shoulder roll to the right, tumbling six feet away from his original position. Gunshots aimed at the muzzle-flash of the M-10 were off target, and James was already giving the enemy another reason for concern.

James fired three rapid shots from the Nambu, pointing the pistol in the general direction of the snipers in the ruins. He ran past McCarter's new position and dove to the ground.

Then McCarter bolted forward, fired his weapon and dropped to the ground. James followed and repeated the "leapfrog" advance. The snipers failed to figure out the tactic, and the Phoenix Force commandos managed to reach the building.

They darted through the pitted, weather-worn threshold to the ruins. The Briton blasted a long salvo of Ingram rounds into the surrounding shadows to force the enemy to stay down long enough for the Phoenix pair to run for the cover of a crumbled brick wall. McCarter ejected the spent magazine and shoved in a fresh 32-round magazine.

"Well, we made it so far," the British ace commented.

"Yeah," James replied as he fed a fresh seven-round magazine into his Colt Commander. He began to reload the Nambu pistol with a magazine he'd taken from the dead Green Tiger *kobun.* "A sniper is perched along the girders at what used to be the second story of this building."

McCarter nodded. "And we've got another bastard running around on this level. I think that a third bloke managed to climb up to the dome."

"Sure hope that's all of 'em," James commented as he worked the slide of the Nambu pistol to chamber the first 9 mm round. He was glad the weapon was a Type 57 Nambu because its mechanism was almost identical to the Colt autoloaders he was used to.

"Any bright ideas about how we're going to handle this without getting our heads blown off?" the Briton inquired.

"How about the old magician's trick?" James replied, taking a penlight from his pocket. "Get the audience to look the wrong way when you pull the stunt."

"Give it a try, mate," McCarter said. "We'll find out if it works."

James snapped on the small flashlight and tossed it to the right. The penlight hit the dusty half-rotted floorboards and rolled across what was left of the room. A burst of automatic fire immediately erupted, and bullets splintered the boards near the flashlight as the beam continued to move with the motion of the rolling pocket torch.

While the light drew the attention of the enemy gunmen, James and McCarter bolted around the left side of the wall. The Briton spotted the muzzle-flash of the enemy weapon from the framework of girders and old wooden beams above them. Snap-aiming his

M-10, he triggered a 3-round burst. The gunman screamed and slipped from his perch to drop to the bottom floor. Rotted boards snapped under the weight and force of his fallen body.

McCarter headed for another jagged block of brick and mortar. Worm-eaten wood gave way under his boot, and his foot burst through the floorboards. The Briton cursed as he fell forward.

The accident saved McCarter's life as he sprawled beneath the path of a trio of bullets fired by a second assailant who suddenly appeared from behind a thick pillar.

James quickly fired at the gunman's position, triggering the .45 Colt pistol. As his right arm rose with the recoil, James fired the Nambu in his left fist. The first bullet chipped the corner of the pillar and forced the man to duck instead of getting full cover. The 9 mm slug tore into his shoulder, and the impact staggered him into the open where James shot at him again with the Colt Commander. A big 185 grain hollowpoint smashed into the enemy gunman's stomach. A Type 64 assault rifle dropped from his trembling fingers as he doubled up from the terrible burning agony in his belly. James fired the Nambu to blast another 9 mm parabellum through the top of his opponent's skull.

A loud creak of timbers strained to the level of protest, alerting James to a threat overhead. The black man whirled and dropped to one knee as he raised both pistols toward the sound. A figure stood along two parallel beams that extended from the base of the dome. The man held a CAR-15 rifle in his fists, the muzzle pointed at James.

Calvin James fired both pistols just as David McCarter triggered a 3-round burst. Parabellums ripped through the enemy gunman's groin. A slug punched a hole through a lung, and a 9 mm round pierced his heart. The bullet-ravaged body seemed to hop from the beams, convulsing wildly in midair, and plunged lifeless to the floor below. Boards caved in, and dust rose around the corpse.

"You okay, man?" James asked McCarter as he approached the British warrior.

"Just turned my ankle a bit," McCarter answered, limping toward the CAR-15 dropped by the fallen gunsel. "Did we get all of the bastards?"

"I think we cleaned house," James declared as he walked to another body to gather up the Type 64 assault rifle. "But our buddies still have some problems to take care of."

Katz and Ikeda had managed to keep the enemy at bay, but James and McCarter realized that their partners were running low on ammunition. Moving to a position directly overlooking the trees near the tomb, McCarter and James aimed at the two gunmen who kept the Phoenix leader in check.

Full-auto death blasted their targets, picking off the enemy triggermen.

The wail of sirens screeched from the streets as several police cars raced to the scene. The hoodlums at the van realized that their comrades were all dead and the odds were just about to turn overwhelmingly against them. The surviving hit men climbed into the van.

"Bastards," James hissed as he aimed the Type 64 and glared through the sights.

The blade of the front sight bisected the window at the driver's side. The profile of a grim-faced Japanese hood appeared as the man reached for the steering wheel. James squeezed the trigger. A hole appeared in the center of the window, surrounded by a network of jagged cracks in the glass. The man's head disappeared from view.

Three police cars arrived as a pair of gun-wielding thugs emerged from the van. One of the cars came to an abrupt halt when the driver saw a thug swing a Shin Chuo Kogyo chattergun toward the prowl car. The gunman sprayed a wild burst of 9 mm slugs. The windshield exploded, and the driver's body jerked in a hideous death spasm behind the wheel.

Two policemen emerged from another police car, 12-gauge riot guns in their white-gloved hands. They didn't hesitate to use the shotguns after they saw what had happened to the officers in the first car. Both shotguns roared, and two blasts of buckshot smashed the machine gunner.

The last thug ducked behind the van, a Nambu pistol in his fist. He realized he had two choices—surrender or death. He chose the latter, and jamming the muzzle of his pistol under his chin, pulled the trigger. A parabellum slug pierced the hollow of his jaw, split the roof of his mouth and burrowed into his brain.

"Mr. Sekizawa?" Katz began as he knelt by the Green Tiger Clan *oyabun*. "It's over now. Safe for you to get up."

"Thank you," Sekizawa replied as he sat up. "I am most impressed by how you and your men handled this situation."

"Impressive isn't the word for this," Ikeda Ken remarked, still breathing heavily from exertion and stress. "This sort of unfettered bloodshed and violence is most disagreeable. I won't be surprised if my superiors decide to have you all thrown out of the country after this incident."

10

"I am sorry, sir," the doll-like young Asian woman with the pretty face explained as she sat behind the reception desk and smiled up at the visitors. "Mr. Kaiju does not answer his telephone."

"This is not a social call or a business meeting," Ikeda Ken reminded her. "I am with Kompei, and my companions are Interpol agents. Kaiju-*san* may be in a great deal of trouble, but that situation will be far worse if he refuses to see us."

"But Kaiju-*san* has not answered his telephone all morning," the receptionist replied, still smiling as if posing for a toothpaste commercial. "Perhaps he left his office without notifying my desk."

"Great," Gary Manning muttered. "The bastard probably skipped town after he heard what happened in Hiroshima last night. Probably figured he might catch some heat."

"Things are getting pretty hot for all of us," Calvin James replied grimly.

The firefight in Hiroshima had indeed upset the Japanese authorities in general and Kompei in particular. Ikeda Ken had come to the defense of the commandos from the United States and insisted that they must be very close to uncovering something that could be a major threat to the safety and security of the Japanese people.

The evidence of a possible war between major yakuza clans alarmed Ikeda's superiors. The fact that three police officers in Hiroshima had been killed was even more alarming. The yakuza traditionally go to great efforts to avoid violence against the police, but the gang who attacked Phoenix Force and Sekizawa Sato were obviously not playing by the rules. The authorities reluctantly agreed to give Ikeda and Phoenix Force forty-eight hours to find whoever was responsible for the carnage.

Phoenix Force still had no information about John Trent or whether the American ninja was involved in the TRIO operation. However, they had solid evidence that the Kaiju Clan was connected with TRIO, and the best lead to the Kaiju yakuza was Kaiju Hideo himself.

Yakov Katzenelenbogen, Gary Manning, Calvin James and Ikeda Ken had come to the import-export office building to bring in Kaiju. James was prepared to use scopolamine if necessary to get him to talk. TRIO was playing hardball, and Phoenix Force was prepared to play just as hard.

"Are you certain Kaiju came in today and went up to his office?" Katz inquired as he noticed four burly figures in business suits who were also headed toward the receptionist's station.

"Quite certain, sir," the woman insisted with a nod. "Perhaps you would like to leave a message?"

"No thanks," Katz replied. "I think we'll go up to Mr. Kaiju's office and check on him in person."

"Excuse me, sir," one of the muscular men in a gray imported suit began. "We gather you have no appointment with anyone here. We ask you to leave before we must ask security personnel to remove you. Please, do not cause disturbance. *Hai?*"

"Kompei," Ikeda explained, showing his identification to the head thug. "Where can we find Kaiju Hideo? Do you know if he is in his office?"

"I do not feel I need to discuss this," the man answered.

"Look, man," James told him, "we're gonna find your boss whether you help us or not. Even if you throw us out of here, Kompei and the Tokyo police will be crawling all over this joint in ten minutes. Even if we're dead it won't change anything 'cause they're gonna raid this place if they don't hear from us."

"We're going up to Kaiju's office," Katz added. "And I hope you're not stupid enough to get in our way because that can only make matters worse."

"I shall accompany you," the thug declared with a curt nod. "My name is Tazaki. Please to come with me."

Tazaki escorted them to the elevator, and they rode the elevator to the tenth floor. The police had finished examining Kaiju's original office after the recent violent incident so the boss had moved back into his regular executive quarters.

The grim-faced hood led them from the elevator, down the corridor to the front office. Tazaki spoke to the pretty secretaries in Japanese, asking if Kaiju-*san* had left his office. They shook their heads in reply. James noticed that the secretaries also wore the same mindless smile as the receptionist downstairs. Kaiju seemed to like his female employees to be attractive, polite and not very bright. Or maybe the ladies had just decided the best way to get along with Kaiju was to smile a lot and pretend not to see or hear anything they were not supposed to know about.

Tazaki knocked on the walnut door to the main office. There was no reply. The big guy turned the knob and opened the door. He uttered a startled sound as if he had just been kicked in the stomach. James and Manning quickly pushed past Tazaki and entered the office, their hands poised at the lapels of their jackets in case they needed to draw guns in a hurry.

The spacious office was still as handsome and well-furnished as it had been when John Trent had visited the yakuza boss. The furniture was back in order, and there was no trace of bloodstains in the carpet. Kaiju Hideo sat behind his desk, his hands braced on the Plexiglas top. His posture was rigid, his head tilted back across the top of the backrest.

A line of dark bruises formed a circle around his neck. James hurried to the desk and put two fingers on the man's neck, but he found no pulse. He examined the marks and noticed the bruises were set close together, but separated.

"He's been strangled," James announced. "Looks like he was garroted with a chain. Expert job, too. Whoever did it got him from behind while he was in the chair. Must have been quick 'cause Kaiju didn't seem to put up much of a struggle. He's been dead for a couple of hours, at least.''

"How could this happen?" Tazaki said with astonishment.

"Kaiju-*san* clearly had enemies," Ikeda remarked. "We already knew this from the incident that occurred only two days ago. Kaiju lied to the police about that incident. Perhaps you can tell us the truth, Tazaki-*san*?"

"I cannot help you," the hood declared. "I know nothing."

"A lot of that going around," Katz commented dryly.

Gary Manning had moved to the window. He pushed aside the curtain and discovered that the latch to the window had been jimmied open. Scratches on the metal frame suggested it had been done from the outside. He opened the window. The walls were smooth concrete, and there was no ledge or stone ridge or balcony. The roof was four stories above.

"My guess is somebody hung a rope from the roof, climbed down and forced the window," Manning declared. "Gutsy son of a bitch, that's for sure."

"I must call security!" Tazaki exclaimed, reaching for the black and white phone on Kaiju's desk. "The killer may still be in the building!"

"I doubt it," Calvin James mused. "The dude who did this is probably long gone by now."

"Go ahead and call security," Ikeda told Tazaki. "And call the police, as well. Tell them Kompei will supply them with written statements about how we discovered the body. However, I think we'd better leave now."

"Wait..." Tazaki began lamely as the four men headed for the door.

"Say goodbye to Mr. Kaiju for us," Manning told him as they left the office.

Ikeda checked with the secretaries to see if someone had entered the office to visit Kaiju earlier that morning or if the women could report any suspicious noises or voices in the boss's office. Katz, Manning and James were certain this effort would lead nowhere. They were right.

"Well, gentlemen," Ikeda said with a sigh as they stepped into the elevator, "do you think the Green Tiger Clan had Kaiju assassinated, or did TRIO become upset with him and order his death?"

"Maybe neither," James remarked. "From what I've seen of TRIO, they don't send just *one* guy to carry out an assassination. Criminal syndicates usually send a hit team, not just a lone hit man, regardless of how good the guy might be."

"Standard procedure for an assassination by virtually any clandestine organization is to use at least three people for the job," Katz confirmed. "The lone-wolf professional assassin is more a colorful figure in fiction than reality. Generally, one or more personnel carry out the actual termination. One or more others provide distractions, serve as lookouts and possibly dispose of the weapons to avoid the killers being caught with the evidence on their person in case there were witnesses. Usually someone else is ready to help with the escape.''

"Well,'' Manning began, watching the different numbers light up on the panel of the elevator as they descended to the lobby. "So far, the evidence suggests Kaiju was killed by one man. Maybe the Green Tiger Clan like to do things different.''

"A silent professional kill by a person who vanishes without a trace,'' James commented. "A job carried out by someone with special skills and training. That doesn't sound like the yakuza. I think Kaiju was killed by a ninja.''

"Trent?'' Manning stared at James. "You think John Trent killed Kaiju? Why?''

"But Trent belongs to the Kaiju Clan. Correct?'' Ikeda inquired. "Why would he kill his clan leader?''

"Trent is a member of the Kaiju Ninja, not the yakuza,'' James insisted. "I never believed the theory that Trent was working for gangsters, and I still *don't* believe it.''

"We did discuss that the previous incident that occurred at this building could have been Trent's work,'' Katz allowed. "Half a dozen thugs killed by pistol and sword. Trent could have done it, and he could have been responsible for Kaiju's death. But why would he do it?''

"Hell,'' James said with frustration. "I don't know, but maybe Trent came here to Japan for an entirely different reason than to start working for the mob. We were sent here to find out if Trent had become a hit man for the yakuza. Anything wrong with the idea that he might be innocent?"

"A man who has killed seven people is hardly innocent," Ikeda muttered as the elevator doors slid open.

"We've racked up a higher score than that since we've been in Japan," James said with a shrug.

"I did not say *you* were innocent," the Kompei officer replied. "However, I understand your meaning."

They stepped into the lobby. Uniformed security officers were arguing with some yakuza thugs about what to do next. The four men walked right past the quarreling group and left the building. They waited until they were outside to continue the conversation.

"Maybe Calvin is right," Katz stated, "or maybe not, but either way it's a pretty safe guess that Trent *is* mixed up in this mess one way or the other. We're still coming up with more questions than answers, and time for this mission is running out fast. We'd better find out if Trent is friend or foe, and we'd better find the answer soon."

11

"Welcome, Kaiju Matso," Wang Tse-Tu greeted as he sat on his great throne within the elaborate command center hidden in the obscure temple. "Welcome to TRIO."

"I am most honored," Kaiju Matso replied as he knelt before the three supreme leaders of the most powerful criminal organization of the Orient.

"We share your loss this day, Kaiju-*san*," Shimo Goro declared. "The death of your brother by treachery sorrows us, as well."

"And the murderers of Kaiju Hideo will not escape our bloody justice," Tosha Khan added. "Just as the monsters who murdered my son shall pay for their crime with their lives."

"There is comfort to be found in just revenge," Kaiju replied solemnly.

Kaiju Matso didn't intend to tell TRIO that he wasn't particularly grieved by the death of his older brother. Kaiju Hideo had always been greedy, selfish and ambitious, with little regard for the lives of others. Matso knew the difficulty of loving a person who seemed incapable of feeling the same emotion or giving it in return, and he doubted that his brother ever really cared about anyone or anything except himself and his own ambitions.

Matso, however, was also a selfish and self-serving individual who found it easy to recognize shortcomings in others but not in himself. Matso lacked his brother's drive and stamina. The younger brother had always been willing to ride on the coattails of his more ambitious and harder-working sibling. Although Hideo may never have truly loved his brother, he had always tolerated Matso and saw to the needs and welfare of his lazy and ungrateful relative.

Kaiju Matso had been the second in command of the Kaiju Yakuza Clan only because he was Hideo's brother. The younger Kaiju had no head for business, no skills for commanding men or coordinating major criminal operations. Matso had basically collected money from the gambling and prostitution branches of the clan. He was even too lazy to try to steal any of the profit, and Hideo always gave him enough to live comfortably, which was all Matso ever really cared about anyway.

The profits from the yakuza operations had served him well over the years. Matso had a fine home in Osaka, a former film star for a wife and a gifted Thai call girl for a mistress. Accountants and lawyers took care of investments in stocks and real estate for the Kaiju family. Matso had planned to retire from clan involvement and live on the legal income from these investments.

However, Hideo's death had thrust Matso into the role of *oyabun* of the Kaiju Clan, a position he was

poorly suited to assume. Yet, he had been contacted
by two TRIO henchmen who informed him of his
brother's death and promptly escorted the startled
Matso to the TRIO headquarters at the isolated temple.

"You know little about us, Kaiju-*san*," Shimo remarked. The leader of the Snake Clan yakuza laid a
hand across the hilt of the *katana* propped against the
arm of his chair. "But you know all that you need to
know at this time. More shall be revealed to you later.
It is enough that you understand *we* are now control-
ling your clan. You will take orders from us. Understood?"

"*Hai,*" Kaiju answered. He recalled that he was
supposed to speak English while in the presence of the
TRIO heads. "Yes, I understand."

"Also understand that your enemies are now our
enemies," Tosha Khan declared. "The men who killed
your brother must now answer to TRIO. In fact, we
have decided to remain here in Japan until this matter
is settled. Blood for blood."

"Do you know who killed Hideo?" Kaiju Matso
asked.

"We are certain it was either the work of the Green
Tiger Clan or another enemy...." Wang Tse-Tu hesitated, not wishing to say too much. "Someone you
know nothing about, yet an enemy potentially far
more dangerous than the Green Tiger Clan."

Matso paled when he heard the news. He was well
versed with how dangerous and ruthless that particu-

lar clan could be, and the idea of confronting an even more dangerous opponent was hardly a comfort.

"However," Tosha Khan added quickly, glaring at Wang from the corner of an eye, "we intend to deal with them. You have no reason to fear."

"In fact, we think you should remain safely out of harm's way until this matter is resolved," Shimo told Kaiju Matso. "We realize you are not accustomed to dealing with the...unpleasant chores associated with this sort of business."

"I appreciate that," Kaiju replied with relief.

"Besides," Tosha Khan added, "you are more a weak link in our organization than a strength. We don't want you getting in the way or breaking down and talking to the authorities if things get difficult."

Matso didn't know what to say to that, so he simply nodded in reply. TRIO obviously knew him for what he was, and they had no faith in his ability to command the clan.

"You will move into your brother's home," Shimo stated. "No one will look for you there. We are also giving you additional protection. Very good men will see to your safety."

"Thank you," Kaiju Matso said, although he realized the TRIO agents would be on hand to watch him and make certain he didn't endanger the organization's interests. Protecting Matso would be a secondary concern, if indeed they were concerned about that at all. "I am in your debt."

"Yes," Tosha Khan declared with a cold smile. "And you'd do well to remember that, Kaiju-*san*."

CALVIN JAMES STROLLED through the crowded streets of Tokyo. Buses, cars and motorcycles shuffled along the four-lane road on Namiki-Dori. The city seemed bigger and more crowded than James recalled from the days when he visited Japan while on liberty during his tour of duty with the United States Navy in Vietnam.

Japan had seemed like paradise compared to the terrible conflict in Southeast Asia. The American had wondered how it would feel to return to Tokyo after so many years. He had expected the memories to be exaggerated, but Japan was still very pleasant and colorful. Tokyo was as crowded as New York City, but the streets were cleaner, and the people remained polite and considerate even when they crowded together to get in or out of public-transportation vehicles.

The other members of Phoenix Force didn't know James had left their safehouse to set out into the streets alone. Katz would probably give him a royal ass-chewing when he returned. They would all be upset with him. TRIO had a contract out, and somehow the super crime network had managed to get a good enough description of each Phoenix Force commando to have them all on the hit list. Venturing out alone was dangerous.

James hadn't taken the risk lightly or decided to slip away from the others without good reason. He wanted to see someone privately, someone who might be able to lead him to John Trent. James was convinced that Trent wasn't working for the yakuza, but he needed proof.

None of the men of Phoenix Force wanted to believe that Trent was a hired assassin, but the others didn't know Trent as well as James did. The former SWAT cop from San Francisco had guessed wrong about men in the past, but his gut instinct told him he couldn't be so wrong about Trent that he could misjudge the man completely.

Yet, he realized Trent had kept a lot of secrets over the years. James hadn't known that the quiet Japanese-American martial-arts instructor was actually a highly trained ninja warrior until Trent had first assisted Phoenix Force in a mission against TRIO in San Francisco. James had never suspected Trent's uncle was a yakuza dealing in black-market goods. Did Trent have another secret, one about his true allegiance, buried away behind the personality that James thought he knew so well?

If James found Trent and learned that his friend was actually an enemy, he would probably have to kill him—if he could. James figured he was probably better with a gun than Trent, but he wasn't sure he could take the ninja unarmed. Calvin James had a third dan black belt in tae kwon-do, and he had been a contender for the Golden Gloves as a youth, but Trent's training in *ninjutsu* included at least a dozen martial arts, with weapons and without.

James had decided to take all the risks involved in trying to locate Trent. He recalled that Trent had mentioned a man named Makino Kita who owned a restaurant called the Higashikaze, the East Wind. Makino was a former sumo wrestler, once a contender for grand champion. He opened a restaurant after he retired.

On one occasion Trent had told James how he'd become friends with Makino during a visit to Japan a few years ago. Makino had toured the United States and liked to talk to American martial artists, so he and Trent had a lot in common. Sumo wrestling is more than two big fat guys bumping bloated bellies: it is a ceremonial martial-art form based on centuries-old traditions.

Sumo requires enormous dedication and years of training. Apprentice wrestlers begin training at the average age of twelve. Boys join a sumo stable where they work as servants and cooks and housekeepers to the older students and more advanced wrestlers. Discipline is extremely strict and training is very harsh. Most recruits don't last long enough to participate in their first professional match.

A sumo must be able to perform splits like a ballet dancer and still be large enough and heavy enough to take on opponents who might weigh more than four hundred pounds. Yet agility, knowledge of leverage and strategy are as important as size and weight. A sumo must be able to hit like an NFL lineman and still be as nimble as a professional dancer. Few men can combine these abilities and fewer still achieve true recognition as a sumo wrestler.

If he succeeds and reaches this level, the sumo becomes an honored and respected celebrity in Japan. He is invited to social functions, and to be seen in his presence is a status symbol of importance.

However, the career of any professional athlete is relatively brief. Most sumo wrestlers have never had an opportunity to develop other job skills besides knowing how to wrestle, cook and clean house. The majority of former sumo wrestlers become restaurant owners or run house-cleaning services. These businesses tend to be quite successful because even a former sumo wrestler is a celebrity in Japan.

The East Wind Restaurant seemed to be doing pretty good business. James finally located the establishment near the corner of Namiki-Dori and Annex Avenue. A bright red sign with yellow letters in English and Japanese ideograms bore the legend of the East Wind. Nearly all signs in Japan are written in English as well as Japanese, and English is the most common second language among Japanese.

The restaurant featured a pleasant combination of Asian and Western styles. Customers could choose tatami mats at a traditional floor-level table or sit Western-style in chairs at a table with a hardwood floor under their feet. The East Wind Restaurant reflected Japan itself, a nation with a proud history and great traditions, yet a very modern country that had incorporated the advantages of the West into its own culture.

"Hello, sir." A middle-aged woman in a kimono greeted James at the door. "I regret to say all tables are presently occupied. Perhaps you would care to wait at our sushi bar until a vacancy is available."

"Thank you," the tall black man replied. "But I would like to speak with Makino-*san*. Is he here?"

"He is busy with business matters, sir," she stated.

"Would you tell him I need to talk to him about a mutual friend named John Trent?" James asked.

"Trent?" She nodded. "I shall relay the message, sir. Please to wait at sushi bar."

James agreed and moved to a set of leather stools along a teakwood counter. Raw fish had never been a great favorite of the Chicago-born commando, and he had to be awfully hungry to consider eating uncooked octopus or eel. He ordered something that resembled whitefish and some sake while he waited for Makino to reply to his message.

He didn't have to wait long. A huge figure appeared next to Calvin James. The man was six feet tall and weighed at least three hundred pounds, yet he carried his massive bulk with ease and grace. His big frame was clad in a black kimono jacket and *hakama* trousers. Shoulder-length black hair framed his smiling moon face.

"Good afternoon," he announced. "I am Makino Kita. I am told you are a friend of John Trent. He is also good friend to me. How is John? I hope he is well."

"That's what I have to talk to you about," James answered, bowing to Makino. "Privately."

"I have not seen John for more than two year now." Makino frowned. "Is he in trouble?"

"I'd rather not talk here," James insisted.

"Ah," the former wrestler said with a nod. "Of course. Please to come with me."

James followed Makino through the restaurant into a narrow corridor. They passed the rest rooms and moved to a private office at the end of the hall. Makino unlocked the door and had to turn sideways to step inside. James followed, and the sumo shut the door. The office was furnished with a heavy oak desk, a set of filing cabinets, two folding metal chairs and a pair of lamps on bamboo end tables.

"Now it is private, yes?" Makino said with a smile.

"Thank you," James replied with a nod.

"You're welcome." Makino returned the nod and suddenly slammed the side of his hand into the black man's stomach.

James doubled up with a gasp, taken off guard by the unexpected attack. Makino moved with uncanny speed for such a large man. He seized James's right wrist and twisted it into a painful arm lock and with his other hand reached inside James's jacket to draw the Colt Commander from shoulder leather.

The Phoenix pro's left hand shot out and grabbed Makino's fist before the pistol could be turned against its owner. James pressed Makino's thumb joint against the walnut grips of the pistol and pried the index finger away from the trigger. He stomped a heel into Makino's instep, making the wrestler groan with anger and pain.

James twisted hard and the pistol fell to the floor. Makino released the wrist lock and suddenly wrapped his thick arms around the American's narrow waist. James's feet left the floor as Makino easily lifted him in a bear hug. The black commando raised his hands to clap the open palms against his opponent's ears, but Makino turned swiftly and released the black man.

Calvin James hurtled across the room and crashed into an end table. The lamps fell off and shattered on the floor. His ribs felt as if he had a knife in his side. It was only the corner of the end table, but Makino was thundering forward, powerful hands poised for attack.

James grabbed the small table and lashed it across Makino's arm. The sumo wrestler grunted and moved back. James rose to his feet, holding the table as a shield. Makino smiled and nodded.

"What the hell . . ." James began.

"I make you eat table—" Makino scowled and further displayed his knowledge of English "—son from bitch."

He stepped forward. James raised the table toward the sumo's face. As Makino lifted his arms to ward off the attack, James swiftly rammed the table into his opponent's barrel chest. The man grunted and staggered back a step. James slammed the table across Makino's left shoulder to try to keep his opponent off-balance.

Makino lashed out with his right hand in an open-palm stroke that ripped the table from James's grasp, following the swipe with a cross-body karate chop aimed at the neck. The American ducked under the whirling arm and swung a right *seiken* punch to Makino's massive belly and a left hook to the his side. The thick layers of flabby muscle protected the wrestler like body armor, and James realized he had made a serious mistake.

Makino confirmed this. He seized James's jacket and used it as a handle to raise the American off his feet once more, then spun around and hurled him across the room. The black warrior slammed into a wall and slid to the floor in a dazed heap. Makino stomped forward and reached down to grab his stunned opponent.

James braced himself against the floor and launched a powerful tae kwon-do kick to Makino's chest. The sumo groaned and stepped back two paces, and James leaped to his feet to square off with his huge adversary. Makino smiled thinly and prepared to attack.

The Phoenix commando raised his arms to distract Makino and hooked a kick to his ribs. His foot seemed to bounce off without effect. Makino charged, and James lashed out with his other foot in a roundhouse kick aimed at the big man's face. The wrestler spun around from the blow, and James planted a flying-jump kick between his shoulder blades. Makino fell forward, his bulky belly slamming into the desk.

Makino grabbed the telephone from his desk, turned and threw it at James's head. The American ducked to avoid the projectile, and Makino charged forward. The sumo's cheek was bruised, but otherwise he didn't seem to be any worse off than when the fight started. James wished he felt the same way.

The wrestler closed in. James jabbed him on the chin with his left and altered it to a hook punch to the jaw. Makino's head jerked from the blows, and James swung a hard right cross, but his forearm was seized. The huge man turned abruptly to haul James off-balance, and the American once again found himself flying across the room.

"Shi-i-i-t!" James cried as he tumbled across the desk to sprawl on the floor.

"Kita!" a voice snapped. "Stop that!"

"Huh?" Makino said distractedly.

James picked himself up and leaned against the desk, breathing hard. He felt as if he had been used as a volleyball for six games straight. Blinking to clear his vision, he stared at the tall slender figure standing next to the sumo wrestler. John Trent looked back at him steadily.

"What the hell are you doing here, Cal?" Trent asked.

"Gettin' bounced off the walls mostly," James replied as he walked unsteadily from behind the desk. "Do the human tank and I have a truce now or what?"

"If you are friend of John—" Makino smiled and wiped some blood from the corner of his mouth with the back of his hand "—you are my friend, too."

"I thought I told you that before we came back here and you started using me for a *makiwara*," James stated.

"Excuse, please," Makino said. "I noticed the bulge of gun under your jacket. I thought you were enemy of John who claimed to be friend. You understand?"

"Yeah," James said with a nod. "It's okay. I guess neither of us really got hurt."

"It was good fight, anyway. You hit real damn hard. Yes?"

"You don't do so bad yourself, pal." James turned to Trent. "We gotta talk, John. In case you didn't know it, you're in a lot of trouble."

"I don't understand," Trent replied. "Why are you in Japan? Oh, God. Are your four friends here, too? This isn't a very good time to recruit me for one of your missions."

"This time *you're* the mission, John. At least, that's how it started. The direction of the mission has gotten a little confused 'cause a lot happened over the last two days."

"A few things have happened to me, too," Trent said with a sigh. "I think we'd better talk."

12

Phoenix Force had set up a safehouse in Tokyo at a storage house a half a mile from the famous Senga-kuji Temple. The graceful curved rooftops of the temple, surrounded by tall evergreen trees, were visible in the distance.

But the graves of the fabled forty-seven *ronin* buried at the temple were not visible from the warehouse. The *ronin*—samurai without a master—had avenged their murdered warlord against overwhelming odds. Then they had committed *seppuku*—ritual suicide by cutting open the belly—generally known as hara-kiri by Westerners. The incredible courage and supreme sacrifice of the forty-seven warriors is greatly honored and admired by the Japanese.

But Phoenix Force wasn't concerned about Japan's historical sites and were relieved when Calvin James returned relatively unharmed—except for the bruises acquired during his fight with Makino—and they were very surprised to see John Trent with him. But there were unanswered questions.

Rafael Encizo gathered up a Heckler & Koch MP-5 machine pistol. He didn't think Trent presented a threat, but the Cuban veteran had been betrayed too

many times to assume that Trent was totally trust-
worthy without some evidence to dismiss the suspi-
cions that had brought Phoenix Force to Japan.

Gary Manning was leaning against a large wooden
crate, his brawny arms folded on his muscular chest.
The Canadian's right hand rested on the grips of the
Eagle .357 Magnum autoloader in shoulder leather
under his left arm. David McCarter sat on one of several sofas in storage, his right foot propped up on a
coffee table, with a wet cloth wrapped around his
swollen ankle. The Briton's M-10 Ingram rested in his
lap, but that wasn't unusual for McCarter, who never
liked to be unarmed.

"Glad to see everybody's still here," James remarked, glancing somewhat sheepishly at the ap-
proaching Phoenix leader.

"They are *now*," Katz answered. He drew James
aside for a minute, glaring at him. "Wandering off by
yourself wasn't very professional, Cal. You could have
gotten yourself or some of us killed if we went looking for you."

"I know," James admitted. "But I was pretty sure
I could find John if I went alone. If we all went looking for him, the odds would have been too great that
somebody would have recognized us. It was a calculated risk, but it was worth it."

"Did Cal tell you why we were sent to Japan?" Katz
asked, turning to the American ninja.

"Oh, yes," Trent confirmed. "You thought I might
be working for the yakuza. Something about an auto
corporation vice president who was murdered with an

American-made *tanto* knife. Afraid I haven't read the papers lately. I've been rather busy, but I assure you, I didn't join the yakuza. Quite the opposite, in fact.''

Trent explained how he had confronted Kaiju Hideo to try to convince him to allow his uncle Inoshiro to retire from the Kaiju Yakuza Clan because the old man didn't want to get involved in narcotics and prostitution.

"Kaiju refused, and he told his men to kill me," Trent continued. "Well, I was forced to kill some of them instead. You know about that already. Anyway, I had to flee and plan my next move."

"Did you strangle Kaiju in his office this morning?" Katz asked directly.

"Yes, I did," Trent admitted without remorse. "Kaiju Hideo would have arranged for my assassination and my uncle's. He would have killed me if I didn't get him first. It may not legally qualify as self-defense, but my conscience has no problem accepting what I had to do."

"No argument," Katz said with a shrug. Long ago, he had learned that justice is not always possible through courtrooms. "What do you intend to do now?"

"Hideo's younger brother, Kaiju Matso, must also die before I can safely leave Japan," Trent answered. "He will have an obligation to carry out blood vengeance against me and my uncle for the death of his brother. He will also be obliged to carry out the final plans that Hideo intended to follow through in order to show the followers of the clan that he is worthy of respect and honors the policies of his slain brother. These obligations are known as *geri*, an obligation and a burden that must be accepted and acted upon if a man is to live as a man."

Gary Manning stepped closer. "What do you know about the Kaiju Clan's connections with TRIO?"

"I didn't know there was any connection until now," Trent replied. "But it explains why the Kaiju Clan has suddenly decided to get involved in narcotics instead of the relatively harmless black-market trade. If TRIO is involved, my task will be somewhat more difficult."

"You think you can defeat all of TRIO?" Encizo remarked. "We've come up against them on three previous occasions. You were with us on two of those missions. We haven't even come close to nailing the leaders."

"TRIO has floating headquarters," Manning added. "The leaders set up an operation and head somewhere else. Fact is, we may never find out who's really behind them."

"Well, that's not our mission," Katz stated. "We were sent to find out about Trent. We've done that. Technically, our mission is finished."

"What the hell, Yakov," McCarter began, shifting his foot from the coffee table. The Briton gritted his teeth when his foot touched the floor. "Are you saying we're just going to leave now? What about TRIO and the yakuza gang war?"

"That's really a problem for Kompei and the police," Manning reminded the eager Briton.

"Yeah," agreed James reluctantly. "But we sort of stirred things up worse than they would have been if we'd never shown up in Tokyo. Kinda feel responsible for that."

"We took out a lot of TRIO thugs," Encizo remarked. "That might slow them down at least. Let's face it, there will always be criminals, terrorists and all the rest. We can't get rid of them all."

"Yeah," James stated. "But some cops got killed in Hiroshima because they backed us when we encountered an ambush during our meeting with Sekizawa."

"The men who did that are already dead," Manning said with a shrug. "Don't give me a bunch of crap about hunting down the men who hired those cop killers. TRIO didn't intend to have any cops killed when they sent those hit men to the Memorial Park. Either Sekizawa or we were the targets, and the police were simply in the wrong place when the bullets were flying. There's no conspiracy to kill cops here. This is a gang war between hoods. That means *both* sides are bad guys."

"But Sekizawa is clearly the lesser of two evils," James insisted. "You told him that yourself, Yakov."

"Sekizawa Sato? The head *oyabun* of the Green Tiger Clan?" Trent inquired. "He is an honorable man for a yakuza—and the yakuza actually follow a code of conduct. I would hesitate to call it 'honor,' but at least there are certain principles involved."

"I can't help feeling that we'd be leaving a job half-done if we left now," McCarter declared. "You know, it's possible we could find a solid lead to the top men in TRIO if we can get our hands on the right people this time.''

James paced about. "I've got a feeling this could be the big one. If we can shut down TRIO, that's gonna put a big crimp in the heroin traffic throughout the whole world. It will set back criminal activities of all sorts not just here in Japan, but every place TRIO operations extend to—including the United States.''

"We could check with Ikeda and see if he needs any help," Katz announced. "We owe the guy a favor or two after all the help he's given us during this mission. He's also taken a lot of heat because of us, and we might be able to get his superiors off his back if we can prove this was all worthwhile.''

"That's better," McCarter agreed cheerfully as he stood, trying to conceal the pain in his ankle. "I say we go for it.''

"And I say get your weight off that ankle," James ordered. "You've got a sprain, and you could end up not going anywhere.''

"Nag, nag, nag," the Briton muttered, but he resumed his seat and put his foot back on the table.

Katz looked at each of them in turn. "What do the rest of you say?''

"If we can do some good," Manning said with a nod.

"Any opportunity to finally crush TRIO is fine with me," Encizo agreed. "We could also check with Seki-zawa again. He's got connections within the yakuza underworld, and he might have new information that could help.''

"You already know how I vote," James declared.

"I'd like to assist, as well," Trent offered. "My loyalty is to the United States, but I was born and raised in Japan, and I love this country. TRIO threatens both nations. This is my fight, too."

"All right," Katz declared. "We'll find out where we stand and what we can do. Then we'll decide what—*if any*—action to take next."

DAVID MCCARTER REMAINED at the safehouse with Encizo while Katz and Manning met with Ikeda Ken at Kompei headquarters. James and Trent had arranged a meeting with Sekizawa Sato.

The news from Kompei was less than encouraging. "The authorities want us out of the country," Katz explained to Encizo and McCarter back at the safehouse. "They know about Kaiju Hideo, but they believe he was killed by the Green Tiger Clan or some other warring yakuza outfit. Gangster or no gangster, Kaiju was officially a respected businessman, president of a major corporation. Ikeda says Kompei believes the best thing we can do is quietly leave and hope the matter resolves itself."

McCarter snorted. "Oh, it will. After bloody TRIO kills off all the competition and runs all the criminal activity in Japan. Don't they realize that TRIO is worse than any yakuza clan?"

"Kompei doesn't think we've made any progress, and they don't like the way we've left bodies lying around ever since we arrived in Japan," Manning said with a shrug. "We're not going to get any help from the local police—here in Tokyo or anywhere else in Japan. In short, gentlemen, we're really on our own now."

"Have we made their Most Wanted list yet?" Encizo asked, only half joking.

"Not yet," Manning replied. "But we're well on the way to achieving it. We've only got about twenty-four hours before they put out an all-points bulletin and come looking for us to place us under arrest if necessary."

"Brognola would be thrilled if he heard we'd contacted the U.S. Embassy to see about getting out of a Japanese prison," Encizo said with a sigh.

"I'm still a British citizen, remember?" McCarter commented. "And Gary's a Canadian. I'm not sure the U.S. Embassy would do us a lot of good."

"I don't think it would come to that," Katz replied. "Kompei would simply deport us back to the U.S., or some of us might have the options to be deported to Great Britain, Canada, or in my case, Israel. No matter which option we take, Phoenix Force is going to be a thing of the past after Brognola finds out we blew it and caused a scandal in the process."

"Naturally," Manning added. "Kompei isn't giving us any more information, either. To put it bluntly, we're screwed."

"But not in all directions," Calvin James announced. He and Trent had entered earlier and stopped in their tracks near the door to listen. "Sekizawa passed on some information that's a lot more encouraging than what you got from Ikeda."

Manning made a sour face. "Never thought we'd be getting help from a Japanese gangster. But at this point any source would be welcome."

"Well, Mr. Sekizawa and his Green Tiger Clan want to settle the score with TRIO as much as we do," James began. "He's pretty pissed because his bodyguards got offed at the park last night."

"Sekizawa is an *oyabun*, and the attempt on his life demands retaliation," Trent explained. "The fact that his bodyguards failed to protect him, yet five strangers—Occidentals at that—succeeded in saving his life reflects badly on the ability of the Green Tiger *kobun*. They feel that they have lost face."

"The big problem for Sekizawa's people was finding a target," James added. "He didn't know where to find the leaders of TRIO, so he ordered his men to go after the next best thing. They planned to assassinate Kaiju Hideo."

"But Kaiju is already dead," Encizo remarked.

"Sekizawa's people didn't know that when they staked out Kaiju's house at the outskirts of Tokyo," James answered. "Anyway, they missed Kaiju Hideo because he'd already gone to the import-export office building where somebody else wasted the sucker. Luckily, I had John with me to fill them in on the details."

"I bet old Seki-saw-saw or whatever his name is was surprised to find out that the bloke who took care of

Kaiju had just waltzed into the room," McCarter said with a grin.

"To say the least," James confirmed. "Needless to say, it also made quite an impression. Sekizawa figures he owes us quite a bit since we saved his life and took out an enemy."

"So what does he plan to do to repay us?" Manning asked.

"He started by telling us what his *kobun* learned from surveillance of Kaiju's house," Trent declared. "Of course, Kaiju Hideo was not in the house, but Kaiju Matso arrived about two hours ago. He was accompanied by a lot of men carrying hand luggage—briefcases, flight bags, canvas tote bags, that sort of thing."

Encizo nodded understandingly. "Just the right size to carry disassembled submachine guns. Sounds like somebody's expecting trouble."

"Wait a minute," Manning began. "These hoods are with this Matso character to protect him, right? So why did they choose Hideo's house? Surely they could have found a less obvious hideout."

"Seems the police would certainly investigate the house for evidence for why Hideo was killed," McCarter added.

"The cops had already been there and didn't find anything," James explained. "They didn't even seal the place off to come back later. I guess they knew enough about Kaiju to figure he didn't keep anything concerning the yakuza at home."

"But why did Matso go to his brother's house instead of hiding out in a damn fishing village on the coast of Okinawa?" Manning wondered aloud. "Even if he isn't worried about the police, you'd think he'd suspect the Green Tigers might have the place staked out. Doesn't sound right to me."

The Israeli had been quietly listening to the others, thinking over the information before contributing to the discussion. "Matso might not appreciate the risk. But TRIO *would* realize either the Green Tigers or we would probably check out Hideo's home. Rafael's right. They expect trouble. In fact they're counting on it."

"Bait," McCarter declared. "The bastards are using Matso for bait to try to lure us into a trap."

"That's what I suspect, anyway," Katz confirmed. "The theory could be wrong, of course, but if it's right, it means somebody higher up on the chain of command for TRIO than Kaiju Matso ordered it. Unless Matso has enough guts to offer himself as potential sacrifice."

"Not according to Sekizawa," James replied. "The old guy says Matso is a real ball-less wonder. A lazy little coward who's been riding along on his big brother's coattails for years. I think your theory's right, Yakov."

"Wonderful," Gary Manning said with a sigh. "We're going to waltz into a trap now. Well, what the hell. We've been getting ambushed by TRIO ever since we started poking around Tokyo. At least this time we know where it'll happen."

"We can also have reinforcements if we want them," Trent added. "Sekizawa has offered to supply us with weapons, transportation, whatever we want. He will also supply men to assist us. His *kobun* are eager to regain face, and Sekizawa, too, is obliged to help us. He owes a great debt to us and, for now at least, we're all on the same side. We all have a common enemy."

"Well, gentlemen," Katz began. "We've got less than twenty-four hours to wrap up this mission. We'd better get to work."

13

"This job sucks," Andrew Tanaka complained as he paced the dense carpet of the spacious living room inside the home of the late Kaiju Hideo. "We have to baby-sit that punk Matso and set ourselves up as a target along with the son of a bitch."

"Be patient, Andy," Harold Kuming said with a smile. The muscular Chinese-American sat in a leather armchair and stared at a television game show on the wide-screen color TV set. The steel balls in his hand clicked methodically to the movement of his fingers. "At least you speak Japanese. I don't have any idea what these other jokers are talking about."

"You're not missing much," the Japanese-American TRIO hood assured him. "Most of them are yapping about baseball."

"Baseball?" Kuming turned to gaze at the Snake Clan and Kaiju Clan yakuza thugs assembled in the dining hall in the next room. "You're shittin' me, Andy."

The late Kaiju Hideo had combined Western and traditional Japanese styles in the decor of his home. Although the living room was furnished like a Hollywood version of a jet-setter's pad, the dining hall reflected Japanese tastes. The yakuza henchmen knelt around the long table set close to the floor. Most of them were playing dominoes, making bets on the plays. A couple of *kobun* who enjoyed a greater intellectual challenge were engaged in a game of *go*. Sometimes referred to as "Japanese chess," *go* is a centuries-old board game of strategy employing a wide checkerboard and dozens of black and white stones.

Some of the yakuza carried pistols in shoulder leather, but most only had a sword beside them on the floor, ready for use. Kuming thought they were passing around the sake bottles too frequently considering the fact that they knew the situation could turn dangerous at any moment. But none of the Japanese thugs seemed to be tipsy.

"Baseball is a national pastime in Japan," Tanaka reminded Kuming. "One of those great traditions we Americans passed on to the Japanese. Along with making cars and radio parts."

"Small world, huh?" Kuming snorted. "I'll be glad to get back to Frisco. To be honest, I'm not very comfortable in this country."

"I know what you mean," Tanaka replied. "My ancestors came from Japan, but I feel outta place, too. I've been here several times before, and I always feel like a fish on the freeway."

"This bait bullshit doesn't thrill me, either," Kuming admitted. "I'm not worried about the Green Tigers. Hell, half the yakuza in Japan still carry swords, and most of the others are so lousy with a gun they'd probably be better off to use a blade instead.

What worries me is the possibility those guys who hit us back in Frisco are gonna do a repeat performance here.''

"Yeah," Tanaka agreed. "Those bastards are just too damn good at killing people."

"You fear five men although we have thirty to oppose them?" Matsuno Sadatoshi demanded as he entered the room. "You should be ashamed to admit this cowardice."

The two Asian-American hoodlums glared at Matsuno. He stared back with a blank expression on his lean features. Matsuno wore a white kimono jacket with matching *hakama* and a bloodred obi sash around his narrow waist. The headband around his skull bore the three-headed serpent symbol of TRIO. He carried the honored *katana* samurai sword of the Matsuno family since the sixteenth century. Matsuno gripped the scabbard in his left fist so he could easily draw the blade with his right. A *wakazashi* short sword and a traditional *tanto* knife with a ten-inch blade were thrust into the sash.

Tanaka and Kuming considered Matsuno to be a fanatic, a lunatic who fancied himself as a samurai hero from an old Toshiro Mifume film. But Matsuno was just another subchief in charge of a bunch of TRIO hoods. Technically, Matsuno's rank in TRIO was no higher than Tanaka or Kuming's, but the native-born Japanese gangster had been chosen to command the operation at Kaiju's house.

The yakuza thugs, especially the Kaiju *kobun*, wouldn't be as eager to follow orders from Americans—even Americans of Asian descent. However, that didn't make Tanaka and Kuming any happier about being subordinated to Matsuno Sadatoshi, who obviously returned their dislike. Matsuno would have preferred never to set eyes on Tanaka and Kuming.

"We're not cowards, Matsuno-*san*," Andrew Tanaka told the Japanese gangster. "But we're not foolish enough to underestimate those mysterious commandos. I seem to recall that you were no more successful against them in the Philippines than we were in San Francisco."

"They were lucky and managed to catch us off guard," Matsuno said grimly. "That won't happen again."

"I'm glad you're so confident," Kuming remarked. "Have you considered the fact that your swords won't do much good against guns? Those guys are experts in small arms, and they've shot your yakuza boys full of holes every time they've tangled with them."

"The only advantage a gun has over a sword is distance," Matsuno said with contempt. "If I am two meters from my opponent, his life will be lost even if he manages to take mine as well."

"What do you do at three meters?" Tanaka muttered as he reached for a bowl of fruit on a glass-top coffee table. "Ask the son of a bitch to hold his fire until you can get close enough to—"

Matsuno's right hand streaked to his *katana*. Sheathed in the side of the scabbard was a small knife, its ornate bronze hilt disguised as a decoration. He drew the diminutive knife and hurled it at the fruit bowl. The blade pierced an orange inches from Tanaka's fingertips.

"Goddamn!" Tanaka cried, jerking his hand away.

"I didn't know you're a Christian, Tanaka-*san*," Matsuno remarked with amusement as he stepped forward to retrieve his knife. "Perhaps you'll want to go to church after this is over."

Tanaka had automatically reached inside his jacket for the 9 mm Nambu pistol under his arm, but he resisted the urge to draw his pistol and put a bullet in Matsuno's mocking face. The time was not right to settle scores with fellow TRIO members. Later, Tanaka thought solemnly, if we're both still alive.

"*Kozuka* throwing knife," Matsuno announced as he plucked the small blade from the orange. "Samurai were taught to use these in childhood. It can be thrown accurately up to four meters. I could have just as easily put your eye out as lanced this fruit for demonstration purpose. Does that answer your question, Tanaka-*san*?"

"Where's Matso?" Harold Kuming asked quickly. He decided the discussion was getting to a level of potential violence and it was time to change the subject.

"He's in the den with a few of my men," Matsuno replied. "I think he's getting drunk. His brother also had a weakness for alcohol. Disgusting that such weaklings can serve as *oyabun* and command other men."

"Hell, Matso isn't in charge of anything," Tanaka remarked. "The three kings of TRIO figured out how to best use that spineless moron."

"Hai," Matsuno confirmed, finally agreeing with Tanaka on at least one subject. "And if the bait is killed in the process, it does not matter. When one is hunting tiger, one doesn't worry about the fate of the goat used to lure the cat into ambush."

"If the enemy doesn't kill Matso, TRIO will get rid of him, anyway," Kuming predicted, staring at the steel balls in his hand as he continued to work them in tiny orbits with his constantly moving fingers. "Little prick knows too much about TRIO, and he's too unreliable. They can't trust him to keep his mouth shut, so somebody will silence him forever."

"I sincerely hope I shall be granted permission to take his head from his shoulders when that time arrives," Matsuno declared. "Now, I must check on the rest of my men."

Tanaka watched Matsuno march arrogantly from the living room. The Japanese-American hood wished he could simply put a bullet in Matsuno's spine right then and there.

"God, I wanna kill that pompous bastard," he muttered.

"Relax," Kuming urged. "Before the night's over, somebody might save you the trouble."

TWILIGHT GRADUALLY GAVE WAY to the darkness of night. Most of the yakuza hoodlums didn't expect any trouble until later that evening when darkness became dense enough to conceal intruders. The guards posted outside the house were bored with their watch, convinced nothing would happen during their shift.

They did notice the helicopter that appeared on the horizon more than a mile from the house, but the whirlybird didn't seem to present any threat as it hovered about in circles in the distance. They would have been more concerned had they noticed it was a U.S. Bell UH-1D military chopper. The Bell was popular during the Vietnam conflict due to its fourteen-man capacity and a range of more than five hundred kilometers.

The sentries watched the helicopter for a while but soon got tired of following its monotonous pattern in the sky. A military defense base wasn't far from the site, and they guessed the chopper was probably on some sort of test exercise. Of course, they reported the helicopter to their superiors. Even Matsuno and the two American TRIO commanders decided the chopper was no cause for alarm as long as it remained far from the Kaiju house.

But the sentries definitely snapped to attention when two army jeeps rolled up the driveway to the Kaiju property. The lead vehicle was driven by a young Japanese dressed in military fatigues and a cap displaying the rank of sergeant. Another Asian sat beside him, clad in a class-A Japanese officer's army uniform. He didn't appear to be much older than the sergeant, although the emblems on the shoulder board of his tunic labeled him as a captain.

Another man, also in fatigues, rode in the back of the jeep. He had a radio headset over his sleek head and frequently turned toward the helicopter to observe it through a pair of field glasses. He seemed taller than most Japanese, and the guards couldn't see his face clearly, but they overheard his fluent and rapid Japanese as he spoke into the mouthpiece of his radio headset and detected no trace of a foreign accent in his speech.

The second jeep was also driven by an Asian in army fatigues, but the passengers appeared to be Occidentals. One man was hunched over in the front seat next to the driver. A heavy gray beard and mustache covered most of his lower face, and a pair of goggles and the turned-down brim of a fedora concealed most of the upper portion.

The other Caucasian in the back seat appeared to be at least ten years younger than the man in the front seat. A bushy mustache covered his upper lip, and he wore black horn-rimmed glasses and a cloth hat with the brim pulled low on his forehead. He was a big man, thickly muscled with wide shoulders and a powerful chest.

The jeeps moved toward the front gate of the Kaiju estate. Two sentries waited for them, their pistols concealed under their suit jackets. Other yakuza thugs lurked in the shadows along the side of the house, submachine guns and sawed-off shotguns in hand. The TRIO hoods weren't sure what was going on, but they hadn't counted on tangling with the Japanese

Army, and naturally they didn't want any trouble with the military.

The officer in the lead vehicle spoke a formal greeting as the jeep came to a halt, its headlights illuminating the two TRIO sentries at the opposite side of the gate. "I apologize for this interruption. I am Captain Ishikawa. Perhaps you can help us?"

One of the sentries inquired about their business.

"Hai," Ishikawa replied with a nod. "You must be curious about what we're doing. Did you notice the helicopter over there?"

"Of course," the hood answered. "It is neither silent nor invisible."

"This is very true," Ishikawa agreed. "You notice how it repeats an orbit over and over again? It moves in circles and seems to be doing nothing at all except burning up fuel. *Hai?*"

"Herr Kapitän!" the bearded man called from the second jeep. *"Was ist das Verduss? Schnell, mein Herr! Schnell!"*

"Warten Sie ein Moment, bitte!" Ishikawa called back sharply. He sighed and turned back to the gate. "Impatient and barbaric lot. Even their scientists are overeager and crude."

"The language you spoke sounded like German," the TRIO thug commented, a little confused and slightly intrigued. "These men are German scientists?"

"Robotics," Ishikawa answered. "I fear I must tell you something that is not totally declassified, but it is not a state secret, either. Those two Germans designed the controls for that helicopter.''

"The helicopter is operated by a robot?" the less talkative hood asked with amazement.

"Actually it is run by a computer system built into the robot drone," Ishikawa explained. "We've been observing the flight. As you can see, something has gone wrong with the robot. Apparently, the computer system has jammed. The programming has failed to feed in the next commands to the drone control center."

"I fail to see why this concerns us," the head sentry declared. Captain Ishikawa didn't appear to be armed, but the sentry wasn't certain that the other men didn't carry weapons.

"When the helicopter runs out of fuel, it will fall from the sky and crash. You have no reason to fear this because you are far away from the orbit of the helicopter. We've come to you for help because you will not be as apt to panic as those within the flight path of the robot aircraft."

"And of course you won't have to risk your lives, either," the yakuza thug said with a cynical smile.

"We need to call the Kogoshi Radio Station," Ishikawa stated. "Professor Muller thinks the computer system to the robot drone is jammed by the frequency of a powerful radio transmission."

"It isn't our problem," the sentry replied with a shrug.

"Please reconsider," Ishikawa urged. "We only wish to use the telephone. What harm can there be in this?"

"I'll ask my employer," the head guard declared. "But he will almost certainly deny you, as well."

"Donnerwetter!" the older Caucasian snapped as he stepped from the second jeep. *"Was ist die Schwierigkeit?"*

"Tell that Nazi fool to shut up," the sentry leader snorted.

"He's not a Nazi," Ishikawa replied.

"He's a German," the sentry said with a sigh. "Germans have never brought anything but grief to Japan. As far as I'm concerned, they're all Nazis."

A sentry concealed among the shadows at the side of the house uttered a gasp of pain and surprise. He slumped along the wall to the ground. The short shaft of a projectile jutted from the side of his neck. Cyanide from the split fiberglass near the steel point immediately entered his blood stream and traveled directly to the brain. He was dead in five seconds.

The other two sentries hidden at that side of the house had been watching the newcomers at the gate. They didn't realize what had happened until they turned and saw their companion's corpse already stretched out on the ground behind them.

David McCarter worked the cocking mechanism of his Barnett Commando crossbow. The British ace placed the shaft of another bolt in the groove along the top of the weapon. He fitted the feathered end of the bolt at the drawn bowstring while the *kobun* peered around, trying to search for the unseen archer and guess where the projectile had been launched from.

Hiraoka Toson, a Green Tiger *kobun* who had accompanied McCarter, poked the barrel of a Type 64 assault rifle through a space in the chain-link fence. A foot-long silencer was attached to the muzzle of the weapon. Hiraoka squeezed the trigger, and a 3-round burst rasped from the T-64.

Another TRIO flunky collapsed before he could aim or fire his Shin Chuo Kogyo submachine gun. The man's weapon slipped from twitching fingers as bloodstains appeared on his dark blue T-shirt. The third gunman aimed his shotgun at the muzzle-flash of Hiraoka's silenced weapon. McCarter had already sighted on the enemy thug's chest by peering through the infrared telescope mounted on his crossbow. The Briton fired the Barnett Commando.

The arrow struck the TRIO sentry in the chest. The steel tip pierced flesh and muscle as the force of the projectile drove the bolt deep to puncture the hood's heart. Cyanide seeped into the wound. With his life pump lanced and poison in his blood, the man was doubly dead and fell to the ground with his finger still frozen in the trigger guard of his shotgun.

"Nice work, mate," McCarter told Hiraoka as he stepped aside to allow a pair of Green Tiger *kobun* to attack the fence with a pair of bolt cutters and a crowbar.

"You shoot arrows good also," Hiraoka replied with a nod.

"I'm just warming up," the Briton remarked with a wolfish grin.

The steel wires were quickly snipped through, cutting open a portion of the barrier. The crowbar was used to pry back the section and provide an opening large enough for the four men to crawl through, one at a time.

THREE MORE TRIO THUGS were positioned at the opposite side of the house. Distracted by the men at the gate, the thugs didn't notice Calvin James and two Green Tiger *kobun* at the fence. Dressed in black camouflage fatigues, Calvin blended well into the darkness beyond the fence. He crawled to the wire, an M-16 assault rifle cradled in the crooks of his elbows. The Green Tiger allies followed his example and crept on their bellies with weapons braced across their arms.

All three men carried 5.56 mm weapons with silencers attached to the threaded muzzles of the rifles. They slid the sound suppressors through gaps in the fence and aimed with the assistance of Starlite scopes mounted on their rifles. Thanks to the optic fibers used in the special lenses, the Starlite allowed them to see blackest night as mere dusk. Since the Starlite magnified faint reflected light to detect objects, it was better than infrared because the night sniper didn't have to worry about being blinded by the muzzle flash of his own weapon.

James and the *kobun* under his command aimed carefully and opened fire. Full-auto bullets hissed from the silencers. Every round was a head shot. Their skulls shattered, the enemy sentries fell as large portion of their brains were plastered against the side of the wall.

Calvin James felt his stomach muscles knot as he stared at the three dead men. Killing opponents in self-defense didn't bother him. That was easy to justify, but he could never get used to taking out enemies like this. But James realized it had to be done. The sentries hadn't gotten a fair fight, but the odds against Phoenix Force weren't fair, either. James could accept what he had to do, but he realized that if he ever "got used to it" he would have good reason to be worried about himself and what sort of person he had become.

"Okay," James told his companions. "Let's go."

The Green Tiger *kobun* with James began to cut through the fence with bolt cutters. Just then, two enemy yakuza appeared from the rear of the house and spotted James's group about to penetrate the fence. The TRIO pair ducked into the shadows along the side of the house. One man pointed his submachine gun at the wire while his partner raised the antenna of a walkie-talkie and prepared to report the invasion to Matsuno.

Neither man noticed the shape that crept silently behind them. Rafael Encizo and two Green Tiger members had climbed over the back of the fence while the guards were preoccupied with the "soldiers" at the front gate. Encizo gestured for the others to stay back. The Cuban drew his Cold Steel Tanto and advanced quietly.

Encizo held the knife in an overhand grip, the six-inch steel blade jutting from the bottom of his fist. He decided to take out the man with the subgun first. The Cuban's arm swung, and the sharp tip of the Tanto struck the TRIO gunman at the base of the skull. The blade split bone and severed the spinal cord as it sunk into the medulla oblongata.

The enemy died instantly. His comrade turned sharply and glimpsed the handle of the Tanto knife, still lodged in the base of the dead man's skull. The survivor dropped his two-way radio and reached for a pistol inside his jacket. Encizo's hand descended down to the hoodlum's face to deliver a hard karate chop across the bridge of his nose.

Stunned, the TRIO flunky fell on his back. Encizo pounced on the fallen man and landed on his chest with both knees, all his weight behind the blow. The sentry gasped breathlessly, and Encizo swung another karate stroke. The side of his hand struck the thug across the neck, crushing the windpipe. Pinning the body to the ground, Encizo waited until the final convulsions ceased. Then he rose from the dead man and pried his Tanto from the skull of the other corpse.

Encizo and his companions joined James's group as they cut through the fence. They hadn't heard any shots or shouts from the other side of the building, so they assumed McCarter's unit had successfully taken out the sentries at the east wing.

A hoodlum near the front door heard dry leaves rustle under the weight of a footstep. He turned toward the sound and was confronted by Calvin James and two Green Tiger *kobun* armed with silenced rifles. Three streams of automatic fire coughed, and the man's body twitched wildly from the impact of nine 5.56 mm rounds crashing into flesh simultaneously.

Another hoodlum nearby cried out fearfully a split second before a crossbow pierced the back of his skull.

The Green Tiger *kobun* who had called himself "Captain Ishikawa" dropped to the ground as the two TRIO henchmen at the front gate turned to see their comrade collapse. The head sentry reached for a Nambu pistol under his jacket. But the "German scientist" with the bushy gray beard had already raised his left arm. A SIG-Sauer P-226 autoloader was clenched in his fist.

The pistol coughed twice through its nine-inch sound suppressor. Two 9 mm parabellum slugs tore into the chest of the head sentry, both rounds burrowing through his heart. The TRIO thug wilted to the ground as the second sentry by the gate drew a Smith & Wesson .38 from shoulder leather.

John Trent had been seated in the back of the first jeep, pretending to operate the communications radio. He now held a short bamboo bow with the bowstring drawn back and an arrow notched and ready. The American ninja snap-aimed and released the feathered butt of the arrow. The missile streaked between the iron bars of the gate. A steel hunting point punctured the sentry's chest, just above the breastbone.

The arrow, like the bolts of McCarter's crossbow, had been treated with cyanide. The poison took effect rapidly, and the TRIO hoodlum died on his feet, the unfired .38 revolver still clenched in his fist. The man collapsed across the corpse of the head sentry.

Gary Manning tossed aside the horn-rimmed glasses and gathered up an FAL assault rifle, equipped with a Starlite scope and a silencer. As he sat in the back of the second jeep, the Canadian marksman raised the FAL and peered through the scope to follow the progress of the last outside sentry who fled toward the front door.

The crosshairs of the scope found the man's shoulder blades. Manning held the weapon steady and waited for the thug to get a little farther. The back of the man's head bobbed into the crosshairs, and Manning squeezed the trigger. A big 7.62 mm slug smashed through the man's skull. He died midstride and fell at the foot of the stairs.

The Green Tiger *kobun* who were dressed in military uniforms quickly drove the jeeps into position, placing the front fenders against the gate. Manning helped them unfold a twelve-foot steel ladder and place it against the fence. Trent buckled a pistol belt around his waist with a .45 Colt pistol holstered at his right hip. The American ninja thrust a *ninja-do* sword through the belt near his left hip. He patted the pockets of his field jacket to reassure himself that his other *ninjutsu* weapons were ready for immediate use.

The Green Tiger *kobun* carried swords, too, but were also equipped with an assortment of firearms. Most of the swords were cheap imitations of *katana*, with crude wooden handles wrapped with adhesive tape for a better grip, but Ishikawa carried a genuine sixteenth-century *katana* made of superb steel.

Yakov Katzenelenbogen used the trident steel claws of the prosthesis attached to the stump of his right arm to tear the phony beard from his face. Manning tossed the Uzi submachine gun to the Phoenix Force commander as Ishikawa and Trent climbed the rungs of the ladder to the top of the gate and hauled themselves over the other side.

At last, the entire assault force was inside the fence. They had already discussed the strategy for the raid. Manning, Encizo and half of the *kobun* headed for the rear of the building. Katz, James, Trent and Ishikawa would enter through the front. McCarter and the remaining yakuza allies would remain outside to cover the exits in case any of the enemy tried to escape.

"You know, I do my best work at close quarters," McCarter complained as he limped toward Katz and James.

"Not when you're slowed down with a swollen ankle," Katz replied. "Stay out here and watch the doors and windows. You have the flare gun, so you can signal the helicopter pilot and let him know when we're ready to move out."

"I've got it," McCarter assured him. "You chaps take care of yourselves."

"We will," the Phoenix commander answered. "Don't fall asleep out here. This isn't a milk run. And watch out for the police. If they arrive before we're finished, we'll be in a lot of trouble."

"What should I do if the cops do show up?" the Briton asked.

"Fake it, man," James replied as he took a concussion grenade from his belt.

"Hmph," McCarter snorted. "Thanks a lot."

14

Calvin James hurled the concussion grenade through a window near the front door. Yakov Katzenelenbogen threw another blaster through the window at the opposite side of the doorway. Glass shattered, and alarmed voices called out inside the house. The Phoenix Force commandos and their allies hit the ground and covered their heads as the door burst open and a TRIO gunsel armed with a Shin Chuo Kogyo submachine gun stepped across the threshold.

The concussion grenades exploded. Glass and framework burst from the windows. The enemy yakuza was thrown off-balance by the blast and hurled headfirst down the front stairs. His weapon clattered along the walkway as he sprawled on the ground in a dazed heap.

Ishikawa rose and swiftly drew his *katana*. The Green Tiger *kobun* rushed forward and swung his flawless steel blade. The TRIO gunman's head rolled away from its owner's body as a tide of a scarlet flowed from the neck of the decapitated corpse.

Calvin James charged through the doorway, followed by John Trent. They entered a hallway, littered with stunned and unconscious TRIO hoodlums. One of the enemy reached for an Ingram machine pistol on the floor. James stomped a boot heel into the nape of the man's neck. The seventh vertebra cracked, and the man slumped, as lifeless as a bear rug.

A dazed TRIO goon staggered from the living room. Blood trickled from his nostrils and mouth. His eyes were glazed, and he seemed disoriented by the concussion blast. Trent snap kicked him in the abdomen. The ball of his foot struck hard, and the guy doubled up with a choked gasp, then Trent followed up, slugging him behind the ear with the barrel of his Colt pistol.

Katz and Ishikawa entered the hall as two TRIO killers appeared at the top of a flight of marble stairs leading to the second story. Both men were armed with submachine guns, but Calvin James and Katz opened fire before the enemy could trigger their blasters. Full-auto rounds tore into the TRIO hitmen. Their bodies recoiled from the impact and tumbled lifeless down the stairs, blood seeping from bullet-ravaged flesh.

James drew an M-26 fragmentation grenade from his belt and jogged halfway up the stairs. Katz and Ishikawa followed, their weapons aimed at the head of the stairs. James pulled the pin from his grenade and popped the spoon. He counted off two seconds before throwing the minibomb.

A figure appeared at the top riser with an American-made M-3 submachine gun in his fists. Katz's Uzi erupted with a well-placed trio of 9 mm parabellums, and Ishikawa fired his Shin Chuo Kogyo a shred of a second later. The enemy triggerman's face vanished as the Uzi blasted away his nose, burrowed through an eye socket and drilled a crimson spider in his forehead. Ishikawa's projectiles ripped into the chest of the gunman. The guy was already dead, but the second salvo of high-velocity missiles drove his body backward to fall across the floor of the upstairs hall.

James lobbed the grenade. It sailed over the body of the slain machine gunner and landed somewhere in the second-story hall. The two Phoenix pros and their Green Tiger ally ducked and covered their heads with an arm. Alarmed voices cried out above them an instant before the M-26 exploded.

Plaster dust, chunks of wood and a severed human arm showered down on James, Katz and Ishikawa. The yakuza ally hissed something in Japanese as he shoved the bloodied dismembered limb from his shoulder. The two Phoenix Force veterans charged up the stairs to the second floor. The mangled remains of at least two TRIO hoodlums were splattered across the hall. The enemies had been blown to pieces by the exploding grenade, and it was difficult to tell from the ravaged parts how many men had been present. Neither Katz nor James cared to examine the gory debris closely enough to determine the answer.

A door opened, and the barrel of a Type 64 assault rifle jutted from the opening. James swung his M-16 toward the door and triggered a 3-round burst. The Japanese rifle fell to the floor, and its dead owner collapsed across it. James flattened his back against the wall and withdrew the exhausted magazine from his M-16. Katz and Ishikawa covered their partner as

James reached for a fresh magazine from an ammo pouch on his belt.

Another door opened, and Katz turned to see Matsuno Sadatoshi raise an arm to hurl his *kozuka* throwing knife. Simultaneously two sword-wielding enemy yakuza charged into the hall. James hadn't reloaded his M-16, and Ishikawa was reluctant to use his subgun for fear of striking the black warrior at such close quarters.

James raised the barrel of his rifle to block a sword stroke and quickly rammed the hard plastic buttstock under his attacker's ribs. The TRIO swordsman groaned and staggered from the blow. James whipped up the M-16 to use the steel frame as a solid bar against his opponent's wrists, making the sword fly from stunned fingers.

The black warrior from the Windy City promptly snap kicked the TRIO thug between the legs. The man gasped in agony and started to fold up from the blow. James smashed the stock of the M-16 across the man's jaw and slammed the barrel down on the dome of his skull. The thug collapsed unconscious at James's feet.

Ishikawa had drawn his *katana* and attacked the other enemy swordsman. Steel clashed. The TRIO thug stepped back and swung an overhead stroke. Ishikawa parried the attack with his own blade and deflected the other man's weapon. The Green Tiger *kobun* lunged, the longer blade of his *katana* stabbing his opponent in the solar plexus. Sharp steel plunged upward, slicing into the chest cavity. The man died twitching against the long blade.

Katz had immediately dropped to one knee, pointed his Uzi at Matsuno and raised his prosthesis to protect his face as he triggered the weapon in his left fist. The *kozuka* streaked from Matsuno's fingers even as two 9 mm parabellums smashed into the TRIO henchman's chest. The knife struck Katz's mechanical right arm. Metal struck metal, and the *kozuka* glanced off harmlessly from the Israeli's prosthesis.

Matsuno fell against the doorway. Blood oozed in twin streams from his chest and formed two red stripes on his white kimono jacket. He held the honored *katana* of his family in his left hand, but didn't attempt to draw the long blade. Matsuno gazed up at Katz and slowly slumped to his knees. He gently placed the sword on the floor.

"An artificial arm," Matsuno chuckled, then choked on blood rising from his throat. The swordsman spat it out. "It appears you've won."

"You're dying," Katz informed him. "I doubt if you'll tell me anything about TRIO's headquarters."

"It would not be honorable," Matsuno replied. He turned toward Ishikawa. "You? Will you grant me a favor?"

"Hai," the Green Tiger *kobun* answered as he gripped the hilt of his *katana* in both hands. "I know what you wish, and I shall oblige you this request."

"Arigato," Matsuno said through clenched teeth. He fumbled for the handle of the *wakazashi* short sword in his sash.

Katz aimed his Uzi at Matsuno in case the man attempted a final attack on his opponents, but the Israeli didn't think Matsuno planned to use the sword against them. The wounded TRIO agent drew the *wakazashi* and kept the point aimed at his own abdomen. James felt his stomach convulse as he realized what Matsuno was about to do.

"Oh, man," James whispered. "I don't wanna watch this."

"But he wants witnesses," Ishikawa declared. "*Seppuku* is an honored act of cleansing one's self of shame and failure before embracing the karma of death. Such an act should be seen and spoken of and remembered."

"No matter how hard you try to forget," James muttered.

Matsuno spoke softly in Japanese. Ishikawa nodded and raised his *katana* overhead. Matsuno managed a weak smile and suddenly plunged the point of his short sword into his lower abdomen. James flinched as he watched the blade sink deep into the TRIO swordsman's belly, but he was also fascinated by Matsuno's self-control. The man had driven nearly a foot of sharp steel into his own intestines, yet didn't utter a sound.

Matsuno's eyes bulged, and his lips trembled with pain as he gripped the handle of the *wakazashi* in both hands and dragged the blade from left to right. The razor edge slit open his belly. Globs of bloodied intestines poured out onto the floor. The stench was almost as terrible to bear as the witnessing of the ritual suicide. Matsuno's body shook from the monstrous agony, but he didn't cry out.

Ishikawa's *katana* struck swiftly. The blade cleaved through the stem of Matsuno's neck, cutting muscle and bone with a single smooth stroke. Matsuno's head tumbled forward and toppled down the stairs. His body sprawled across the disemboweled guts while more blood spewed from the severed arteries of his abbreviated neck.

"Christ," James rasped and looked away from the gruesome sight. His stomach trembled, but he had seen many terrible scenes of death and mutilation before, and he knew he wouldn't vomit now.

"I'm glad that's over," Katz said with typical understatement.

"He died very well," Ishikawa remarked. He snapped his wrist to flick the blood from his sword. "Better than he lived."

James was surprised to hear the retching sound of a man throwing up. Although he, Katz and Ishikawa had ample reason to barf for a week, none of them had responded to the *seppuku* demonstration in this manner. James thought the sound might be his imagination, then he realized it was coming from the door to another room.

"Hey," James whispered as he drew his Colt Commander and pointed at the door with the barrel. "We got a sensitive type tossing his cookies in there."

Katz and Ishikawa stood clear of the door. James stepped next to the doorway and swung a boot heel into the door, just below the knob. The door burst open and revealed a small bathroom. A man knelt by the toilet, his head dangling above the rim of the bowl.

He raised his head weakly. Fear shone in his tear-moist eyes.

"Well, gentlemen," Ishikawa said with a smile. "Look who we found. Allow me to introduce you to Kaiju Matso."

"Are you sure?" Katz inquired with a frown. The frightened, sickly man huddled by the toilet bowl hardly looked like the *oyabun* of a yakuza clan.

"Quite certain," the Green Tiger *kobun* assured him. "I saw Matso with his brother in 1984 when representatives of many yakuza clans met to discuss the end of the clan wars in Tokyo. This is Matso. He doesn't seem to have much stomach for his new position, eh?"

"Dozo," Matso began with a shaky voice. "Please, do not kill me...."

"That will depend on what you can tell us," Katz replied as he pointed the Uzi at Kaiju Matso. "Flush the toilet."

John Trent hadn't followed the others upstairs. He had been busy on the first floor when a number of enemy yakuza attacked from the living room. Two gun-toting *kobun* charged forward. One man fired a big Colt Magnum revolver while the other tried to aim a Nambu Type 14 pistol at the American ninja.

The hastily fired .357 round slashed air inches from Trent. Dropping to one knee, the American ninja aimed his .45 Colt at the attackers. The thug with the Magnum was a bad marksman whose luck had run out. Trent fired the big Colt pistol and blasted a hollowpoint slug into his opponent.

The first gunman dropped unceremoniously to the floor while his partner pointed his weapon at Trent. A relic from the Second World War, the Nambu resembled a German Luger, although some firearms enthusiasts consider it a better made and more accurate weapon than the P.08.

Trent didn't care to find out under the circumstances. He triggered two .45 rounds. One slug caught the second gunman under the chin and plowed through the hollow of his neck to tear open a grisly exit wound at the back of his neck. The Nambu triggerman toppled across the corpse of his slain comrade, but half a dozen more TRIO yakuza rushed forward to replace them.

The remaining gangsters carried swords, not guns. They probably had a bit too much sake and charged into a situation they might otherwise have handled differently, but they still outnumbered John Trent. There were more of them than bullets left in the .45 Colt, too. Trent realized that the gun didn't give him a real edge, anyway. Not at such close quarters. If they rushed him, he might be able to take out two or three before the blades of the survivors would finish him off.

The yakuza formed a horseshoe pattern around Trent, swords held ready, fists clenched around handles poised at stomach level as they sighted across the steel tips at their opponent. They had seen the *ninja-do* in Trent's belt and apparently hoped their opponent would abandon the pistol and use his sword instead. The *kobun* were obviously more skilled with swords than guns, and each man likely fancied himself an expert. They might even take on Trent, one at a time, if he drew the sword. Trent doubted that and knew they would lose interest in fair combat after one or two were felled by Trent's blade.

He smiled at the group and extended his right arm with the pistol in his fist. His left hand slid into a jacket pocket while his right thumb pressed the magazine catch of his Colt automatic. The clip slid from the butt well to the floor. The yakuza smiled and nodded with approval, failing to realize that there was still one round left in the chamber.

Trent pointed the .45 at a grinning *kobun* and fired the last bullet into the man's face. The ninja hurled a *metsubushi* at the floor in front of the yakuza to his left. The eggshell grenade exploded with a burst of flashpowder and black pepper. A blinding light and a small cloud of choking debris hurled up into the faces of his opponents.

Two yakuza attacked from the right as Trent dropped his empty pistol and drew the *ninja-do* from its scabbard. He dodged an opponent's sword stroke, stepped forward and slashed his blade across the side of the *kobun*'s neck. The man went down with blood jetting from a severed carotid artery while another TRIO swordsman swung his weapon at Trent.

The American ninja blocked the attack with the flat of his sword and deflected the blade with a hard shove to the right. He deftly swung his *ninja-do* in a rising sweep and drew the razor edge across the yakuza's throat. The man staggered backward, dropped his sword and reached for the deep slit in his throat. He wilted to the floor as a fourth TRIO killer attacked John Trent.

The *kobun*'s blade connected with Trent's *ninja-do* as another yakuza swordsman rushed behind the ninja to launch an attack from the rear. Trent swung a roundhouse kick to his first opponent's ribs and sent the man staggering, then turned slightly and raised the unsharpened edge of his sword to block the second attacker's blade.

Trent shoved upward and took a circular step forward to the left. The *kobun*'s sword rose, and Trent's blade slashed him across the belly. The man screamed and stumbled forward, blood gushing from the wound. Trent's sword struck again, cutting the man between the shoulder blades to severe his spinal column. The victim's screams ended abruptly, and he fell face first to the floor.

Two opponents remained. One TRIO thug had decided that crossing swords with Trent was not such a great idea, after all. He reached inside his pants pocket and withdrew a small .25 caliber Beretta automatic. He worked the slide to chamber the first round. Trent heard the metallic click, turned and swiftly hurled his sword. The *ninja-do* sailed like a javelin, and the steel point caught the hoodlum under the breastbone. The weight of the thrown sword drove the blade in deep, and the sharp edge sliced through tissue as the handle descended.

The gunman uttered a terrible shriek and fired his diminutive autoloader into the ceiling as he fell to the floor. The *ninja-do* quivered, its tip still buried in the dying man's flesh. But the last yakuza swordsman was smiling as he attacked Trent. The American ninja no longer held a gun or a sword. The thug was certain of victory.

Trent jumped back to avoid the slash of the sword. The opponent quickly thrust his weapon, and Trent sidestepped the lunge. He seized the man's wrists and pulled hard, increasing the forward momentum suddenly, and the man staggered into a sofa. The point of his sword pierced the upholstery, and the blade sunk deep into the furniture.

Trent hooked his left elbow into the enemy's face. The man fell sideways, and his fingers slipped from the hilt of the sword. Trent rammed a *seiken* punch to the solar plexus and lashed the side of his other hand across the upper lip and teeth.

The ninja didn't let up on his dazed opponent. He slammed a heel-of-the-palm stroke under the man's jaw and swiftly grabbed the man's jacket lapels and turned to jam a hip into the hoodlum's abdomen. Trent pulled his opponent onto his hip and adroitly hurled him into the coffee table. The yakuza thug hit the glass top hard. It shattered on impact. The man sprawled unconscious under the framework of the table.

"I hope my uncle appreciates what I've had to go through here," Trent sighed as he started to retrieve his weapons.

GARY MANNING HAD USED four ounces of C-4 plastic explosives to blast open the back door to the house. Rafael Encizo and two Green Tiger *kobun* charged through the doorway. The Cuban warrior sprayed the interior with 9 mm rounds from his Heckler & Koch MP-5. The volley was intended to keep opponents off-balance, rather than kill. It did both.

Three TRIO gunmen had ducked when the explosion tore the door off its hinges. Two others had been killed by the blast. Another yakuza thug had failed to get down and stood directly in the path of Encizo's H&K chatterbox. He caught two parabellums in the kidney area and collapsed.

Encizo and his Green Tiger allies had charged into a large kitchen, complete with stainless-steel electric stoves, a large two-door refrigerator and a counter with a wide top above several cabinets. The Cuban rushed to the cabinets and ducked behind the cover as more TRIO goons charged into the kitchen.

The two Green Tigers dropped to the floor and opened fire on the enemy. One TRIO gunman received four 9 mm rounds in the torso and hurled backward into his comrades. Another was hit in the belly by a burst of double 0 buckshot. Both opponents went down, but four TRIO goons remained.

An enemy *kobun* returned fire with a compact Ingram machine pistol. Parabellum slugs smashed into the forehead of the closest Green Tiger gunman. His skull exploded, splashing blood and brain matter against his companion's arm and shoulder. But the shotgun-toting Green Tiger didn't freeze up or hesitate. He fired the second barrel of his side-by-side 12-gauge weapon and blasted the Ingram gunner with a lethal load of buckshot.

Rafael Encizo braced his MP-5 along the counter of the kitchen cabinets and fired a deadly volley into the remaining TRIO gunsels. An enemy yakuza collapsed, a large portion of his skull blown away. Another fell against a wall, blood oozing from his bullet-torn upper arm. The third swung his submachine gun toward Encizo's position.

Gary Manning carefully aimed his FAL assault rifle and squeezed the trigger. A trio of 7.62 mm projectiles sheared through the bridge of the enemy machine gunner's nose. The back of his skull burst into a minor explosion of blood, brains and bone fragments. The only remaining TRIO gunman had been wounded but still retained a grip on his CAR-15. Not taking any chances with the guy, Manning shot him between the eyes.

The Canadian and two Green Tiger *kobun* entered the kitchen. Encizo emerged from behind the counter and the shotgun-toting Green Tiger rose from the floor to join the others. Manning gestured to two of their yakuza allies.

"Stay here and check the basement," the Canadian instructed. "If it's safe, catch up with us for backup. Be careful about your targets. We don't want to shoot each other."

"And when you join us again," Encizo added, "remember to announce yourselves. We don't want to react before we realize who you are. Okay?"

"Hai," one of them said with a nod. "We understand. Do not to worry."

"We'll try not to," Encizo replied as he, Manning and the yakuza with the shotgun moved on to the next room.

They entered a den. The room featured a large well-stocked bar, leather furniture and a wall of shelves filled with leather-bound books in Japanese, English and French. A painting of Osaka Castle framed by white cherry blossoms hung on a wall. The room appeared to be deserted, but they heard gunshots and shouts of fighting echo from other parts of the building.

"Sounds like the party is still in progress," Encizo remarked. "But we haven't found it yet."

"We found part of it," Manning corrected. "But the rest is going on elsewhere so—"

Without warning, Andrew Tanaka rose up behind the bar with his Nambu pistol in a two-hand Weaver's grip. Harold Kuming and another TRIO killer appeared at the end of the bar. The Chinese-American held a snub-nose .357 Magnum in a ham-size fist as he knelt by the bar and leaned around the corner. His TRIO companion was armed with a British Sterling submachine gun.

Manning and Encizo immediately dropped to the floor and swung their weapons toward the ambushers, but their shotgun-toting ally was a bit too slow this time. Tanaka fired two rounds into the Green Tiger *kobun*'s upper torso and quickly ducked behind the bar. He narrowly missed a stream of parabellum slugs from Encizo's MP-5 that nearly took off the top of his head.

The TRIO thug with the Sterling subgun triggered a long volley, but his skill didn't match his zeal. Most of the bullets ripped into plaster in the wall above Manning and Encizo. Two slugs smashed into the skull of the unfortunate Green Tiger *kobun* with the Phoenix Force pair.

Kuming fired his .357 revolver. A powerful bullet shattered an antique sixteenth-century vase, but scored no other target. Manning retaliated with his FAL and blasted a trio of hastily aimed 7.62 mm rounds in Kuming's direction. The Chinese-American gunman retreated behind the edge of the bar in time to avoid the projectiles. Bullets chewed wood from the corner of the bar and splinters stung Kuming's hand. He nearly dropped his Magnum when the unexpected pain lanced his unprotected flesh.

Encizo triggered another short salvo of MP-5 rounds, exhausting the ammo from the magazine. The TRIO thug with the subgun suddenly dropped his Sterling and tumbled sideways into Harold Kuming. Both men sprawled across the floor and fell into clear view of Gary Manning. The Canadian held his fire because Kuming's revolver slid across the floor, beyond the hoodlum's grasp. The other man was already dead.

"Son of a bitch!" Tanaka snarled as he fumbled with the Nambu pistol's slide. A cartridge had misfed from the magazine and jammed in the chamber. "Hold your fire! I give up, damn it!"

Tanaka tossed out the Nambu pistol to prove he was serious. Manning and Encizo held their fire as the Japanese-American gangster slowly stood, his hands raised to shoulder level. Kuming slowly rose to his feet and held his clenched fists above his head. Manning covered Kuming while Encizo drew his Smith & Wesson M-59 and pointed it at Tanaka.

"Interesting accent," Encizo remarked. "Where'd you learn your English?"

"Where'd you learn yours, spic?" Tanaka replied sourly.

"We're from San Francisco, okay?" Kuming volunteered the information. "In fact, you guys almost got us once before. About three years ago."

"Better late than never," Manning commented as he tilted his head toward a wall. "Get spread-eagled, pal. You know the routine."

"Sure," Kuming said and suddenly thrust his arms forward and opened his fists.

The two steel balls hurled from his hands. Both metal spheres hit Manning's chest hard. The twin blows staggered the Canadian, and he stumbled backward as he triggered the FAL in his fists. The last three rounds spat from the rifle and blasted some plaster from the ceiling.

Kuming lunged forward and seized Manning's weapon. He yanked hard and turned sharply, throwing the Canadian warrior off-balance. Manning hurled awkwardly into a leather armchair, and man and furniture toppled to the floor. Kuming gripped the rifle by its barrel and raised it like a club as he approached Manning.

Encizo started to turn to help his partner. Andrew Tanaka reached for the metal object concealed under the collar of his shirt at the nape of his neck. The gangster yanked the weapon free and lashed out with a two-foot steel chain with iron weights attached to each end. The chain struck Encizo's wrist. One of the weights whirled around his wrist and stung the Cuban's ulnar nerve at the back of the fist clutched around the S&W autoloader.

The pistol fell from Encizo's hand. The chain whirled toward his head. Encizo ducked beneath the slashing iron weight. It brushed the hair at the top of his skull. The chain swung again in a downward arch. Encizo grunted as the weight struck his shoulder muscle before he could back away from the bar.

Encizo recognized Tanaka's weapon. It was a *man-rikigusari*, an ancient fighting chain developed by the samurai as a versatile and potentially lethal weapon. In the hands of an expert, the *manrikigusari* was as deadly as a gun or a knife at close quarters. Encizo had seen John Trent use the chain weapon in the past, and Tanaka seemed to be just as skilled with it as the American ninja.

"Okay, taco-breath," Tanaka growled as he vaulted over the bar, swinging the chain to keep Encizo at bay. "I'm gonna take your greasy ass apart and stuff your head in it after I break that, too!"

He lashed a downward stroke at Encizo. The Cuban dodged the attack, but Tanaka swung the *manri-*

kigusari in a fast figure-eight pattern and delivered another stroke from the opposite direction. Encizo managed to raise an arm to protect his head. Pain jarred his limb as the weighted end struck hard.

Tanaka suddenly dropped to one knee and lashed out with the chain. Steel links spun around Encizo's ankles, and the weighted end locked around the length of the chain. Tanaka pulled hard and yanked the Cuban's feet from the floor. Encizo went down hard. His spine seemed to bounce into his chest from the impact with the floor.

"Eat this, spic!" Tanaka snarled as he raised a foot and prepared to stomp his heel into Encizo's face.

The Cuban's hands flashed. He caught the Japanese-American's ankle and twisted hard. Tanaka grunted with surprise as he lost his balance and tumbled to the carpet. Encizo rolled to his feet and drew the Cold Steel Tanto from the sheath on his belt. Tanaka rose, spinning the *manrikigusari* like a propeller.

"That blade won't help you, you stupid ass!" Tanaka sneered. He smiled confidently as he drew closer, the chain cutting a series of elusive figure eights in the air.

Encizo realized the *manrikigusari* had greater range than his knife. Before he could get close enough to slash or stab with the Tanto, the chain would deflect the attack. He could probably feint and distract a novice fighter and penetrate his opponent's defenses, but Tanaka was too skilled and experienced with his weapon to fall for such a trick.

The Phoenix pro decided on a tactic. It was risky and if it failed he would be in worse shape than before. Encizo assumed a defensive stance and waited for Tanaka to step closer.

Encizo's arm suddenly snapped forward. The Tanto hurled from his hand. The knife wasn't designed for throwing, but Encizo's skill and aim compensated for the unorthodox tactic. The point of the big steel blade struck Tanaka's left foot. The sharp blade pierced his instep and sunk through flesh and bone to puncture the sole of his shoe and bite into the floor beneath.

Tanaka howled with pain and astonishment. Encizo leaped forward before his opponent could recover. He grabbed Tanaka's wrists to prevent him from using the chain and promptly rammed a knee into his abdomen. The gangster doubled up with a groan, and Encizo slammed a karate chop to Tanaka's kidney.

"Spic, huh?" Encizo rapsed as he moved behind his opponent and gripped Tanaka's chain in both fists.

He shoved a knee in the small of Tanaka's spine and pulled hard. The thug bent backward and struggled to retain his grip on the chain. He snapped his head back, trying to butt Encizo in the face, but the Cuban's head was ducked low to avoid such tactics.

Tanaka attempted a back elbow smash. Encizo groaned as the stroke struck his rib cage hard, but he held on and pulled the chain as he continued to bend Tanaka backward. The gangster's fingers slipped from the weighted ends.

Encizo swiftly yanked the steel links across his opponent's throat. He crossed his wrists to tighten the chain around Tanaka's neck. The Phoenix warrior pushed his fists apart and pulled the TRIO hoodlum across his knee. Andrew Tanaka struggled briefly, but the lack of oxygen soon robbed him of his strength. Encizo held the chain taut until his opponent ceased to move. The stench of urine revealed Tanaka had lost control of body functions. He was dead.

Gary Manning had grabbed the chair from the floor and hurled it into Harold Kuming before the big Chinese thug could club him to death with his own assault rifle. The FAL flew from Kuming's grasp, and Manning charged forward, his left fist swinging at the Asian-American's face.

Kuming blocked the attack with a rising forearm stroke and rammed the stiffened fingers of his other hand under Manning's ribs. The TRIO thug's fingers were conditioned by years of *chuan fa*, and the spearhand thrust felt like a knife blade. Manning moaned from the painful blow, and his opponent drove another jab into the Canadian's lower abdomen.

The Chinese-American swung the side of his hand against Manning's skull, and the Phoenix Force warrior fell to all fours, his head throbbing with pain. Kuming kicked him in the ribs and sent him tumbling across the floor. The tough Canadian tried to shove off from the floor and push himself erect as Kuming rushed forward and swung another kung fu stroke.

Manning's forearm met Kuming's wrist to check the attack. He rammed his other fist into the gangster's solar plexus and quickly grabbed Kuming's arm at the wrist and elbow. The TRIO killer attempted to stomp on Manning's kneecap, but the Canadian sidestepped and moved behind his opponent. He twisted Kuming's arm in a firm hammerlock and raised the captive wrist up between Kuming's shoulder blades.

The hoodlum reached back with his free hand and tried to gouge Manning's eyes. The Phoenix pro caught the wrist with one hand and held the hammerlock with the other. Manning shoved a knee between Kuming's legs and drove it into the thug's testicles.

Kuming wheezed breathlessly and moaned from the agony that branched out from his battered crotch. Manning turned sharply and hauled Kuming around to face a wall. The Canadian shoved forward with all his weight and strength. Kuming hit the wall face first. His forehead smashed the glass pane of the framed painting of Osaka Castle. The white cherry blossoms were now smeared with blood.

Manning released his dazed opponent and quickly hammered a fist between his shoulder blades and stomped a foot in the back of a knee. Kuming fell to all fours, and Manning wrapped an arm around his opponent's neck. His brawny forearm locked around Kuming's neck, and his thick bicep muscle pressed into the carotid artery.

Harold Kuming raised an arm to try to defend himself. Manning braced his free hand against the side of his opponent's skull and locked the wrists to form a solid viselike hold. Manning twisted hard. The crunch of vertebrae rewarded his efforts. Kuming's body went limp, and Manning dumped the corpse on the floor.

"There you are," Yakov Katzenelenbogen announced as he entered the den. He glanced at the two battered warriors and the four bodies on the floor. "Looks like you weren't bored."

"Not really," Encizo answered, rubbing his numb arm. "We didn't manage to take any prisoners. Damn near got killed when we tried."

"No problem," Katz assured him. "We got Kaiju Matso himself, and I don't think it's going to be difficult to convince him to sing like a canary. I just hope he's got something worth listening to."

15

David McCarter fired the flare gun into the sky. The brilliant orange light burst within the night firmament, and the Bell UH-1D helicopter headed toward the house when the pilot saw the signal. The chopper lowered to the street outside the Kaiju estate. Phoenix Force, John Trent, the surviving members of the Green Tiger Yakuza Clan and their prisoner climbed through the sliding doors. The Bell whirlybird immediately rose up into the sky once more.

"All right, Kaiju," Katz began as he sat across from the terrified captive. "We're not playing any games with you, and we don't have any time to spare. You'll either answer our questions, or we'll ride this copter to about two hundred yards up and throw you out the door."

"That will be a pleasure," Ishikawa added as he sat with the *katana* across his lap. "A number of my brothers in our clan died because of you and TRIO. Someone will pay for their lives in blood. You have my word on that, you piece of diseased toad scum."

"TRIO forced me to help them," Kaiju Matso replied helplessly. "What else could I do? My brother had made a deal with those three monsters...."

"What three monsters?" Katz inquired.

"The head *oyabun* of the Snake Clan and two other men," Kaiju explained. "I know Shimo Goro by reputation, although I did not think he was still in Japan. The others are a mystery to me, but I think one is Chinese, and one seemed almost Eurasian in appearance. He wore a fierce costume with chain mail and armor."

"The leaders of the Black Serpent Tong and the New Horde," Gary Manning remarked as he fed fresh cartridges into a spare magazine for his FAL rifle. "All three of the kingpins of TRIO must still be here in Japan."

"They won't stay much longer," Calvin James commented. "You can bet your ass they've already learned that we raided Kaiju's house tonight, and since they haven't gotten any cheery news from their boys at the house, they've also guessed how the battle turned out."

"That is almost certainly correct," Kaiju confirmed. "I am sure they will abandon their headquarters as soon as they realize what has happened."

"We don't need a bloody parrot to repeat what we already know," David McCarter snapped. "Where the hell are they? Maybe we can get there before they can pull out."

"That's insane!" Kaiju exclaimed. "You'll be slaughtered!"

"I didn't take a body count back at your brother's place," Rafael Encizo admitted. "But I figure there were about thirty TRIO killers there. Do the kingpins have a larger security force than that?''

"I'm not sure what the odds are exactly," Kaiju Matso admitted. "But the temple is very well defended."

"Where is this temple?" Ishikawa demanded, his fist on the hilt of his sword, ready to draw the blade unless Kaiju talked.

"It's close," Kaiju assured him. "Less than five miles to the west. But they'll expect trouble the moment they see this helicopter approach. You'll never be able to get close enough to land and assault their stronghold. They'll cut you down before you can get across the fence."

"Anything special on the opposite side of that fence?" Manning inquired. "Antiaircraft weapons? Bazookas? Missile launchers?"

"I don't know about any of that," Matso admitted. "But I recall they have a helicopter—very similar to this one—and at least two limousines."

"They'll be able to pull out damn quick," McCarter said with a sigh. "I hoped we'd finally catch the bastards this time."

"We might make it yet, David," Katz mused. "I think you should take over as pilot of this chopper. The fellow who's flying it now is doing a fine job, but we need a combat pilot now."

"Yeah," Manning muttered. "The other fellow probably isn't crazy enough to fly this rig into a battlefield."

"Right," the Briton said cheerfully. "This is my sort of job. Come with me, Kaiju. I need you for directions to the temple."

"Just a minute," Katz said, placing the hooks of his prosthesis on Kaiju's arm to restrain the yakuza chief. "Is there anyone at this temple who *isn't* part of TRIO?"

"No," Kaiju Matso answered, shaking his head with dismay. "Every single person in the temple is directly involved with TRIO. Most are bodyguards and enforcers for the three supreme leaders of the organization."

"Well—" James grinned "—that's gonna make things a lot easier for us."

"Easier?" Kaiju stared at the black warrior as if he suspected the man had lost his mind. "I don't understand."

"There are no innocent bystanders at the temple, and we won't need to pump any of them for information," Katz explained. "That means we don't have to handle this lot with kid gloves. In other words, we're going to simply destroy everybody and everything at the enemy stronghold."

"*Hai!*" Ishikawa said and clapped his hands with delight. "Now we shall put an end to these scum forever. Truly, my *kobun* and I shall regain face with our *oyabun* and repay the debt to your people at the same time."

"But since I'm helping you," Matso said hopefully, "that means you will not include me in this blood vengeance? *Hai?*"

"We're only interested in crushing TRIO," Manning assured him. "Not your Kaiju Yakuza Clan."

"But *I* am still concerned about what you plan to do after this is over," John Trent told Kaiju as he approached the new *oyabun* of the Kaiju Clan. "Our business is not over, Kaiju-*san*."

Trent had changed into his black ninja costume. His head and face were covered by a hood and scarf mask drawn across his nose and mouth. Trent's cotton jacket, trousers, and split-toe *tabi* footgear were all black. He carried his *ninja-do* sword in an obi sash and a .45 Colt on his hip. Other weapons were concealed within the pockets and pouches of his clothing.

"I...I don't understand," Kaiju began, frightened and confused. "I don't even know who you are. What quarrel have you got with me?"

"Perhaps none," Trent decided. "That will be up to you. Certain changes made by your brother caused some personal problems for my family. This was no doubt because of TRIO. If you decide to change these clan policies and remove these problems, I may let you live, after all."

"You two will have to figure that out later," Katz told Trent. "We've got to prepare for one last confrontation with TRIO and we don't have much time to get ready."

THE HELICOPTER APPROACHED the temple stronghold rapidly. The pagoda-style building was surrounded by a tall stone wall and seemed to be an ironic choice for the final showdown with TRIO. The temple had once been a house of worship, but it was now a headquarters for evil. TRIO's roots were also found in the past. The Chinese tong societies had been originally created to organize freedom fighters against Manchurian rule in China more than three hundred years ago. Unfortunately, as the tong began dealing in opium and white slavery to raise money for the cause, it gradually changed into a criminal organization. The yakuza clans had once consisted of *ronin*, mercenary samurai with a reputation like Robin Hood's. They were "thieves with honor" who stole from the upper classes and helped the oppressed peasants of feudal Japan.

TRIO was the ultimate perversion of these original organizations, just as the temple was now a base for crime instead of a place of religion. McCarter worked the controls of the helicopter as he stared down at the ancient stone structure below. The building was only three stories high, and lights were visible in several windows. The gardens and lawns had been replaced long ago with concrete and asphalt. McCarter spotted the TRIO helicopter pad below. Kaiju Matso had been correct. The enemy had a chopper virtually identical to the Bell UH-1D Phoenix Force had borrowed from the Green Tiger Clan.

The rotor blades of the TRIO chopper were turning slowly. The pilot of the enemy aircraft had obviously just started up the engine. McCarter also noted the three cars parked near the entrance of the temple—two limos and a smaller vehicle that McCarter couldn't identify from the air. Several figures darted about between the building and the wall surrounding the temple. The enemy had noticed the Phoenix Force chopper, and they suspected why it was headed toward their stronghold.

"I hope you chaps haven't gone to sleep back there!" McCarter shouted to his companions as he brought the Bell directly over the enemy helicopter pad.

They had to prevent the TRIO aircraft from taking off, and Gary Manning had the solution to the problem. He held a hastily constructed pipe bomb. Only eight inches long with metal caps at each end, the pipe was filled with C-4 plastic explosives. Manning triggered the detonator and hurled the pipe grenade out the open doors of the chopper.

The bomb struck near the TRIO chopper, which was still preparing to lift off. The C-4 charge exploded. The blast ripped into the enemy helicopter and sent the ravaged bodies of three or four TRIO hoods hurtling across the parade field. The chopper burst into a blazing wreckage of twisted metal and charred pieces as flaming gasoline shrouded the landing pad.

TRIO gunmen rushed for cover behind the three automobiles. They used the cars for bench rests to fire up at the Phoenix Force chopper. McCarter had already swung the Bell away from the site, and most of the enemy bullets missed the speeding aircraft. The TRIO gunmen were armed with short-range submachine guns and pistols, but some fired Heckler & Koch or Japanese Type 64 assault rifles with greater accuracy and longer range. A few rounds struck the metal skin of the chopper.

A Green Tiger *kobun* cried out and clutched at the shallow wound on his right cheek. A bullet ricocheting inside the chopper had creased his face as it whined off metal and buried itself in the Plexiglas window at the side of the carriage.

Calvin James fed a cartridge-style grenade into the breech of the M-203 launcher attached to the underside of his M-16. The black commando aimed his weapon at the three cars below and triggered the firing mechanism of the M-203.

A 40 mm grenade streaked from the muzzle of the M-203, descending from the Phoenix chopper like a lightning bolt out of an angry sky. The grenade smashed into the limousine and exploded. Metal turned into shrapnel, and glass was transformed into flying razor blades. Fuel burst from the exploding tank with the surge of a flamethrower.

The TRIO gunsels stationed behind the limo were killed instantly. Others were cut down by shards of deadly debris that traveled with the velocity of bullets, propelled by the force of the blast. Flaming gasoline splashed on a henchman who bolted onto the asphalt apron, fire licking his upper torso and limbs. The man's hair ignited, and the shock pitched him face first to the ground as the flames continued to consume his still form.

The explosion also ruptured the fuel tank of the Mercedes-Benz parked in front of the limo. A searing tongue of heat reached the dripping gas tank and ignited the fuel supply still confined within the vehicle. The second car exploded and hurled forward in a bizarre somersault to land on its top, tires positioned upward like the round legs of an enormous dying insect.

The asphalt apron was laced with burning wreckage and mutilated corpses. The wall surrounding the temple was worthless against an assault from the air and had only served to trap the TRIO hoodlums within their stronghold. A fortress can often be a great coffin, and the trappings of security designed to keep invaders out can lock victims in.

McCarter piloted the chopper in a circle around the temple. TRIO gunman fired at the helicopter from windows and a platform at the rear of the building. Phoenix Force and their Green Tiger allies returned fire with automatic rifles through the open doors of the Bell copter.

Gary Manning continued to use his trusty FN FAL assault rifle with a Starlite scope. The Canadian marksman triggered 3-round bursts, his powerful arms and shoulders accepting the recoil of the Belgian war machine with ease. He skillfully selected targets and picked them off with professional calm.

Yakov Katzenelenbogen usually favored the Uzi submachine gun, but the weapon was designed for relatively close-quarter combat. He had selected another Israeli military weapon for situations that required greater distance. Katz braced the metal stock of the Galil assault rifle at his left shoulder and held the forearm stock with his prosthesis. He squeezed off short bursts with deadly accuracy. The Israeli's skill with a rifle was less impressive than Manning's uncanny ability, but Katz hit most of his targets.

Rafael Encizo personally believed that the best military weaponry is made by Heckler & Koch factories in West Germany. For close work, Encizo liked the MP-5 machine pistol, but he needed a long-range weapon to return fire from the chopper. The Cuban responded with another Heckler & Koch firearm. He fired down at the TRIO gunsels with an H&K 33 assault rifle. The 5.56 mm slugs picked off opponents one by one as Encizo fired carefully and seldom missed.

Calvin James continued to use his M-16, and the Green Tiger *kobun* resorted to an assortment of weapons. Most were armed with Japanese Type 64s or American M-16s, although one of them had brought along a bolt-action .300 Winchester Magnum with a Steiner scope. The Green Tigers didn't have the combat experience and finely honed skills of the Phoenix Force warriors, but they had plenty of enthusiasm and fired a hell of a lot of rounds at the TRIO forces below.

TRIO's people managed to score some hits, as well. A Green Tiger *kobun* carelessly stood in clear view at the sliding doors of the chopper. He caught two enemy bullets in the chest. The man screamed and sailed down in a swan dive to the merciless ground six hundred feet below. Another Green Tiger enforcer suddenly fell backward and landed next to Rafael Encizo. A bullet hole the size of a quarter had been drilled through his forehead.

James loaded his M-203 grenade launcher and dispatched another round of pure destruction. The missile exploded on the platform at the rear of the temple and blasted three TRIO killers into oblivion. James ejected the spent cartridge casing and reached for another grenade.

"Okay," Katz announced. "Let's take the place apart. Remember, try not to bring the roof down because we still need to go inside and make certain we got them all."

Gary Manning reached for a weapon that resembled a sawed-off shotgun with a thick barrel and an enormous muzzle. The device was an M-79 grenade launcher. Manning broke it open and placed a 40 mm cartridge grenade in the breech. He aimed the launcher at the temple and squeezed the trigger.

The grenade shattered a window at the second level of the building. It exploded inside and spewed thermite within the interior of the room. Flames danced at the fragmented window as the Phoenix Force chopper circled around the enemy base. Calvin James fired another grenade from his M-203 and demolished a large portion of an east-wing wall with the high-explosive blast.

Manning and James continued to bombard the temple with grenades. They picked their targets with care and avoided striking at the corners of the structure to prevent large portions from caving in. Several TRIO henchmen bolted from the building but soon discovered there was no place to run. The flaming debris of the wrecked chopper and automobiles left them without cover. Katz, Encizo and Green Tiger marksmen picked them off with automatic rifles while James and Manning continued to fire explosive missiles into the building itself.

McCarter swung a wide arch from the enemy site to allow a clear view of the destruction heaped upon the TRIO stronghold. The enemy had stopped shooting. The building had gaping holes in its walls from the missiles. Fires burned in several rooms at every level of the temple. Nothing moved except the dancing flames at windows and the charred remains of wreckage and corpses on the ground below.

"Chikusho!" Kaiju Matso exclaimed. His face was pale, and he trembled as he stared down at the devastation below. "This is the most terrible sight I have ever beheld!"

"It appears we have killed them all," Ishikawa remarked. Despite his bloodthirsty remarks earlier, even the Green Tiger enforcer had been unnerved by the unfettered fury of Phoenix Force when the elite fighting unit decided to throw out the rule book entirely and strike without mercy. "No one could survive that."

"We have to be sure," Katz replied. He moved to the cockpit. "David, it's time to check the results of our labors. Take us down to the roof. Give us ten minutes inside. If we're not out by then, take off. That's an order."

"I'm not one to run out on my mates," McCarter replied sourly as he worked the collective and turned the cyclic controls. "Could have the yakuza pilot take over now...."

"He's dead," Katz told him. "Getting out of here is your job, David. If we're not out in ten minutes, it means we're never coming out. Take off and save what's left of our group. There won't be anything else you can do."

"Right," the British ace agreed reluctantly. "You blokes be careful. I don't want to have to break in a bunch of new teammates."

Katz joined the others at the fuselage. He turned to Manning and Encizo. "I want you two to remain here," Katz announced. "Gary, you're our best marksman. You may have to pick off opponents if they try to shoot down the chopper."

"Hell, Yakov," Manning complained. "Okay, I'll do it."

"Why do I have to stay?" Encizo demanded.

"Because your arm was hurt when you fought that guy with the chain back at Kaiju's place," Katz answered. "You'll have too much trouble climbing around on the roof. You'd present a risk to yourself and the rest of the team. You'll do more good to us here."

"All right," Encizo said with a sigh.

"That leaves you and me," James told Katz. "And whoever's crazy enough to come along."

"Yeah," John Trent agreed as he stepped forward. "Let's do it."

"I will also accompany you," Ishikawa declared. "And so will my *kobun*."

"Only one or two," Katz urged. "This is the sort of job best done by a small group of good men. Besides, we'll have to get in and get out fast. That's more difficult with a large group of men."

Ishikawa selected two of his men for the job. The helicopter continued its orbit and headed for the roof of the temple. Katz put down his Galil and gathered up his Uzi. James exchanged his M-16 rifle for a Smith & Wesson Model 79 submachine gun, a favorite weapon of the U.S. Navy SEALs. The six men who were going into the temple attached carabiners to their belts.

As the chopper descended above the roof, James slung a coil of rappeling rope over his shoulder and passed another coil to Trent. The ninja nodded to confirm that he understood. James and Trent gathered up some more climbing gear and moved to the open doors of the carriage. Katz rapidly explained to the Green Tiger enforcers what would have to be done on the roof. They nodded in agreement although they seemed less eager to participate than they had been before Katz told them about using the ropes.

James and Trent jumped from the copter to the roof. They landed surefooted at the crest of the roof and moved along the top to a thick support at the center. James hammered a piton into the roof and secured it to the support. He made certain it was firm and attached a CMI rescue pulley to the stake and ran the rope through it. He slid the rope through the carabiner on his belt and held on to the other end of the line. Trent followed his example and prepared the second rope in the same manner.

Katz, Ishikawa and his men joined them on the roof. They linked up to the ropes with their carabiners. James, Katz and Ishikawa hooked up on one line, and the two *kobun* joined Trent on the other. They walked backward to the edge of the roof, and one by one, they went over the edge. They controlled the descent with the pulley line as they lowered themselves to two windows at the third-story level. The glass was already shattered, and they simply kicked out what remained before swinging through to the rooms inside.

Ishikawa gasped with alarm when he stepped on a corpse sprawled near the window. Katz and James joined him in the room and unhooked themselves from the rope. They unslung their weapons and ventured into the hall beyond where Trent and the two Green Tiger allies met them.

Quickly moving from door to door, they checked the rooms on the third floor. Some of the rooms were on fire, and soon the air would be too thick with smoke to breathe. The flames were spreading, and the building would collapse within half an hour if the place continued to burn. They found several corpses, but no living TRIO agents.

The fire was worse at the second story. They discovered two disoriented TRIO thugs in the hallway. The hoodlums were coughing violently and staggering about off-balance, but both men were still armed. Ishikawa spat a curse in Japanese and opened fire with his Shin Chuo Kogyo subgun. Parabellum slugs chopped the life from the TRIO flunkies.

They searched the second-story rooms as best they could, but much of the middle portion of the temple was ablaze. The search team didn't find any more opponents, except for corpses. The biggest threat seemed to be the fire. The smoke was more dense, and the flames were getting worse.

The group moved to the flight of stairs to the last level of the building. Fire crackled throughout the first floor, and the smoke drifted through the hallway like thick fog. James and Katz headed down the stairs first, followed by Ishikawa, Trent and the two Green Tiger *kobun*.

Movement in the billowing smoke caught James's attention. He dropped flat against the risers of the stairs. Katz followed his example, but Ishikawa didn't react quickly enough. Two pistols snarled from the hallway and pumped four rounds into the Green Tiger enforcer. Ishikawa twitched from the impact of the high-velocity slugs and tumbled down the stairs.

Ishikawa's corpse crashed into Katz as the Israeli started to rise. The heavy blow sent Katz hurtling to the floor below with the dead body draped across him. The Phoenix Force commander's skull hit the floor hard. He groaned as consciousness began to fade into a black mist.

Calvin James slid to the bottom of the stairs and poked the barrel of his S&W subgun around the edge of the stair post. He fired a quick volley at the two gunmen in the hallway. One opponent cried out and fell while the other bolted down the hall and ducked into a room.

"Take care of Katz!" James shouted to Trent as he chased after the gunman.

Trent and the two *kobun* descended the stairs. The American ninja knelt beside Katz and Ishikawa to check both men's pulses. Katz groaned softly and stirred slightly. Trent raised his head to inform the two yakuza allies that their commander was dead. But they weren't looking at him. Following their line of vision, Trent saw the man standing near the front entrance of the temple.

"Shimo Goro!" one of the Green Tigers snarled as he tossed his submachine gun aside and reached for the handle of the sword thrust into his belt.

"*Ee-yeh!*" Trent shouted as both *kobun* approached the lone figure who was calmly waiting for them.

Shimo Goro still wore his ceremonial outfit. He carried the *katana* of his family in his left hand, his right hand resting on the hilt. A *wakazashi* was thrust into his scarlet obi next to the green-dragon fan. His hard face was illuminated by the flickering light of the surrounding flames. He didn't seem worried about the two *kobun* who had drawn their swords, ready to attack.

The first Green Tiger enforcer raised his sword and charged toward Shimo. The TRIO ringleader allowed the man to close in and suddenly drew his *katana* in a lightning-fast stroke. Shimo's blade slashed a deep cut across his opponent's belly before the other man could complete his sword stroke.

The second attacker swung his sword as his comrade fell dying. Shimo's *katana* slashed forward to meet his opponent's blade. The superbly crafted *katana* connected with the poorly made yakuza sword of the Green Tiger enforcer. High-quality steel shattered the lesser weapon. The blade snapped in half, and Shimo's weapon descended to split the other man's skull.

"Ninja?" Shimo looked at Trent with surprise. "Do you intend to simply shoot me, or will you also give your life as a gift to me before you die?"

Trent replied by drawing his *ninja-do*.

The two men squared off. Shimo attacked first, his strokes skillful and powerful. Trent countered with his sword, blocking an overhead cut that was quickly followed by a circular slash and a diagonal stroke. Shimo was very fast and a true master of *kenjutsu*. Trent thought it would have been wiser to simply shoot his opponent.

Shimo's left hand streaked to the fan in his obi as he swung the sword in his right fist. Trent blocked the attack with his *ninja-do*, but Shimo lashed out with the closed fan. The steel ribs struck Trent's wrists and sent the *ninja-do* hurtling from stunned fingers. Shimo struck out with the *katana*. Trent jumped back, but the TRIO swordsman's blade slashed a shallow cut across his chest.

The American ninja tried to ignore the pain from the gash in his flesh and the fear that crept into his stomach and threatened to root him in his tracks. He realized he couldn't draw his pistol, thumb off the safety catch and fire it before Shimo delivered a lethal stroke. He reached for the *manrikigusari* at the small of his back instead.

Shimo swung the *katana* in his right fist while he held the steel fan in his left as a secondary weapon. Trent lashed out with the weighted chain. Steel links struck the TRIO gangster's sword and wrapped around the blade. The weighted end locked the chain in place as Trent yanked hard to pull Shimo forward.

The American stepped clear of his opponent's blade and kicked Shimo in the abdomen. The side of his left hand chopped across Shimo's right wrist to strike the *katana* from his grasp. Trent pulled the chain hard and sent the long sword flying across the room.

Shimo's left arm shot out and drove the hard end of his steel fan into Trent's chest. The blow staggered the American and drove him back two steps. Trent swung the *manrikigusari*. The end struck Shimo's left hand and knocked the fan from his grasp, but Shimo immediately drew his *wakazashi*.

The TRIO swordsman swung his weapon. Trent grabbed the other end of his *manrikigusari* to raise the chain as a bar to block the sword stroke. Made of the same excellent steel as the *katana*, the superb blade of the short sword cut the chain in half, its tip raking the scarf mask and tugging it from Trent's face.

John Trent threw himself to the floor and executed a shoulder roll to put some distance between himself and his opponent. He drew a *shaken* from a belt pouch and hurled it at Shimo. The TRIO ringleader grunted with pain as the sharp steel points of the throwing star bit into his chest.

Trent scooped up his *ninja-do* from the floor and attacked the wounded swordsman. Shimo attempted a thrust with the short sword, but Trent unleashed a powerful blow and forced the enemy's blade aside. Trent moved with the motion of the stroke and pivoted in a full circle to deliver a diagonal stroke across the side of Shimo's neck. Blood spurted from severed arteries as Shimo Goro staggered backward and crashed in a dead heap on the floor.

Calvin James approached the door of the room where the gunman from the hallway had fled. The Phoenix Force commando stood clear of the door and prepared to kick it in. The report of a pistol roared within the room. James was surprised that a bullet didn't burst through a panel of the door, but he didn't hesitate and slammed a heel into the door to kick it open.

Tosha Khan turned his head toward the door as he stood over a still body sprawled across the floor. The Mongol saw the submachine gun in James's fists and swung his Nambu pistol toward the black man. James triggered his weapon and blasted a trio of 9 mm slugs into Tosha Khan. The impact sent the Mongol tumbling backward against the armrest of a thronelike chair.

James glanced about with surprise. Black curtains hung from the walls. Brass dragon incense burners were mounted at each corner of the room, and three thrones were placed on a platform facing James. He looked down at the corpse on the floor. The dead man was dressed in an incredible ornate Chinese robe and slippers. A cap with a peacock-feather tassel lay next to what was left of Wang Tse-Tu's head. The Chinese gangster had been shot point-blank in the face.

Tosha Khan groaned with agony as he dragged himself into the chair. The Mongol turned slowly and faced James. Blood seeped from the wounds in his chest, but his eyes still burned with hatred. James kept his M-79 ready in case the Mongol made one last try to kill him before his own life expired.

"Filthy barbarian," Tosha Khan said thickly, nearly choking on the blood that rose up from his throat. "I...I am the descendant of Genghis Khan.... I cannot die at the hands of an African savage."

"Don't sweat it," James told him. "This 'savage' is from Chicago. Why'd you kill your buddy in the Chinese bathrobe?"

"Wang refused to fight," the Mongol replied weakly. "Wanted to...surrender. I executed him for cowardice...."

"Thanks," James declared. "Saves me having to do it myself. Guess you were the leader of the New Horde portion of TRIO. Wang must have been the Black Serpent Tong boss. Where's the Snake Clan *oya-bun*?"

"Go to hell—" Tosha Khan rasped as he slowly slumped from the chair and fell lifeless at the base of the platform.

"Only after you," James remarked as he stepped from the room.

Katz had regained consciousness, James found as he approached the foot of the stairs. John Trent was leaning against the railing post. His black ninja outfit was stained with blood, and he looked as if he might collapse from exhaustion. The fire was consuming more of the building, but the exit out the main door was still clear. They would have no trouble getting out of the temple, and McCarter could hover close enough to the ground for them to climb aboard the chopper.

"Shimo Goro is dead," Trent announced. "So are all the Green Tiger *kobun*."

"The other leaders of TRIO are history, too," James replied. "Give you the details later. We'd better get out of here before our time runs out."

"Two minutes left to go," Katz commented as he checked a Rolex watch he carried in a shirt pocket. "No problem."

They headed for the door and emerged from the temple. McCarter spotted them, and the helicopter began to descend. A few moments later, the Bell UH-1D rose into the night sky with Phoenix Force, Trent, Kaiju Matso and the remaining members of the Green Tiger Clan who had joined them on the final phase of their mission.

The temple continued to burn until the supports of the building gave way. The roof collapsed and the walls caved in, burying the bodies of Shimo Goro, Wang Tse-Tu and Tosha Khan. It was the final funeral pyre for TRIO.

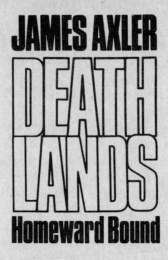

JAMES AXLER
DEATHLANDS
Homeward Bound

**In the Deathlands,
honor and fair play are words of the past.
Vengeance is a word to live by . . .**

Throughout his travels he encountered mankind at its worst.
But nothing could be more vile than the remnants of Ryan's
own family—brutal murderers who indulge their every whim.

Now his journey has come full circle. Ryan Cawdor is about
to go home.

Take
4 explosive books
plus a
mystery bonus
FREE

Mail to **Gold Eagle Reader Service**®

In the U.S.
P.O. Box 1394
Buffalo, N.Y. 14240-1394

In Canada
P.O. Box 609
Fort Erie, Ont. L2A 5X3

YEAH!   Rush me 4 free Gold Eagle novels and my free mystery
bonus. Then send me 6 brand-new novels every other month as
they come off the presses. Bill me at the low price of just $14.95 —
an 11% saving off the retail price - plus 95¢ postage and handling
per shipment. There is no minimum number of books I must buy. I
can always return a shipment and cancel at any time. Even if I never
buy another book from Gold Eagle, the 4 free novels and the
mystery bonus are mine to keep forever.   166 BPM BP7F

Name   (PLEASE PRINT)

Address   Apt. No.

City   State/Prov.   Zip/Postal Code

Signature (If under 18, parent or guardian must sign)

This offer is limited to one order per household and not valid to
present subscribers. Price is subject to change.

                                    4E-SUB-1D